Passage to the Plaza

THE ARAB LIST

Passage to the Plaza

SAHAR KHALIFEH

TRANSLATED BY SAWAD HUSSAIN

Seagull
BOOKS

LONDON NEW YORK CALCUTTA

SERIES EDITOR

Hosam Aboul-Ela

Seagull Books, 2020

Originally published ias *Bab Al-Saha*, 1990
© Sahar Khalifeh, 1990

First published in English translation by Seagull Books, 2020
English translation © Sawad Hussain, 2020

ISBN 978 0 8574 2 770 0

British Library Cataloguing-in-Publication Data
A catalogue record for this book is available from the British Library

Typeset by Seagull Books, Calcutta, India
Printed and bound by WordsWorth India, New Delhi, India

Dedicated to him
Whether near or far
Longing for horizons

This gathering of women was akin to those get-togethers that the deceased would once organize. The dead woman had been in her prime, despite a long line of descendants. She was porcelain white with undeniable fleshy bits, but her waist was well defined and her legs slender. She had been a proud, powerful woman; even so, she was never short of worry when hosting. She would carefully dress herself, spritz perfume, paint her face and transform her house into an Eden of jasmine, myrtle and clove, accentuated by the scent of tobacco wafting from glowing hookahs decorated with bamboo leaves, glass baubles and velvet pipes.

For the occasion, Sitt Zakia had come with one of the have-nots, a woman with a sweet tongue, talkative yet polite, who made the rounds with coffee, serving rings of the sweet delicacy meshabbak and carrying the hookahs. Cradling the hookah in one hand and puffing on the pipe in the other to keep it alight, she scuttled back and forth between the kitchen and the sitting room. Once she reached the intended guest, she would nestle the hookah at their feet, wipe the beak of the hose and fold it into a half moon, whispering, 'Enjoy.'

On one occasion, when she was in her youth, Sitt Zakia had tried to mimic the actions of such a woman. The women had winked at each other, exchanging banter about the length of the hose, how thick it was and how good it tasted. The now deceased had hastened after her, a floating cloud of georgette and perfume pouring forth. She had wrested the pipe from her daughter-in-law's fingers and sniped, 'It's done like *this*!'

'No . . . it's better when it's straight,' one of the women from the far side of the sitting room had countered, and the whole room rumbled with laughter, making the young girl scamper off, dazed and stumbling out of shyness. How could such old, wise and respectable women speak like that? Much later, Sitt Zakia learnt that what they implied, what they had been muttering about, was the law of life itself: the secret of offspring, the thing that preoccupies all women and the livelihood of every midwife. Glory to Him who brings life from death and death from life!

Um Mohammed leant forward with the thermos of black coffee, gave her a teacup without a handle and whispered, 'Hussam wants you. He's in the kitchen.' She rose from her place in the heart of the sitting room and hurried to the kitchen. She found him standing at the window, the North Mountain behind him, glistening in the receding dusk light. What light there was outside didn't allow her to make out his features. He loomed out of the dark like an apparition. He bristled with irritation. 'What's all this, then?'

She held out her hand, anxious. 'Please, not so loud, someone might hear you!'

'Have some consideration for the martyrs' families!'

She placed her hand on her chin—the familiar gesture for a plea—and pled with him, 'Please, we don't want any trouble here.' She peeked out the window, lines of worry creasing her forehead. 'Did anyone see you?'

He smiled and shook his head. 'Is it me you're worried about or the house?'

She didn't answer but kept looking out of the window, murmuring all the while, 'There is no god but God.'

The house was bursting with women who had come to give their condolences; the recitation of the Quran could be heard and the air was heavy with the aroma of black coffee. Hoping to stir his compassion she said, 'After all, she was your grandmother!'

'Of course she was, she was your stepmother, too. She was ninety, she lived a good long life. As for the young people, these days . . . ' he didn't finish.

'Death is everyone's fate,' she said with great conviction.

'And for every death, there's got to be a grand celebration?'

'It's only for seven days.'

'And only three for young people like me!' he grumbled angrily. He flew towards the door and slammed it behind him. Its echo resounded in the silence of the hall, the

Quranic verses being recited and the final rays of daylight. She saw his shadow slip away between the grapevines, snails and cactus arms. She stood still, watching until he was gone. He made his way over the short wall of stacked rocks, across the fence enclosure, under the heather hedge trimmed into an arch, then disappeared among the rocks and thorns, making his way towards the north side of the mountain.

2

'Mama isn't afraid of the dark!' That's what the young men in that neighbourhood told one another, what the masked men whispered whenever she passed through Khan Al-Tujjar, through the squares, back gardens or the backstreets. Before being engulfed by the darkness, she would raise her voice in greeting, 'Assalamu alaikum wa rehmatullah.' God's mercy and peace be upon you. She would then look out of the corner of her eye without turning around. Inevitably, out of the darkness, a masked man would ask her, 'Sitt Zakia, are there soldiers on the road?' Not turning right or left, she would keep on walking and respond, 'The house is safe for man and jinn. God's mercy and peace be upon you!' She would then continue on her way.

One day, she froze at the sound of a shout, 'Stop there!' The soldiers surrounded her, their Uzis aimed at her and her bag.

'Open up.'

She opened her bag and they saw her basic tools: cotton, gauze, syringes, disinfectants and suppositories.

'Doc-tor?'

'No, qabila.'

'Ka-bila? What dat?'

'Midwife.'

'Middle wife?'

'Meaning I help women deliver, bring babies into the world.'

'Bebees! Bebees!'

She heard the word travel on their lips, from one to the next, laughing. But the soldier who had stopped her didn't even crack a smile. 'Put down bag.'

She put the bag on the floor. He took a few steps back, his weapon and those of two others still pointing at her.

'Over turn.'

She looked at him, bemused. In a frenzied voice, he bellowed 'Empty!' His voice made the cobblestones and buildings quake, and the ghosts of the night too. He kicked the bag and backed away swiftly, all the while watching her as she took out her medical instruments, murmuring, 'There is no strength or power but in God, there is no strength . . .'

'What this?'

'Syringe.'

'Singe?'

She clasped the rubber bulb and squeezed it. He took another step back and yelled, 'On ground!'

She placed it on the ground and he kicked it away. She smiled to herself. *They're scared of everything, even syringes . . . all living things . . . even street cats.* At that very moment, a cat strolled alongside the shuttered shop fronts towards the rubbish skip. Sitt Zakia trailed the animal with her eyes as it stepped out of the spot of orange light from the lamp post. She caught sight of black silhouettes behind the skip. Her heart began to beat so wildly that she almost believed she was having a heart attack. What would happen if they started pelting the soldiers with rocks? Or Molotov cocktails? What if both sides went at it and she was caught in the crossfire? Would they really attack each other here, in the middle of the street?

She was still invoking God's name when she reached the house. The pregnant woman was in the throes of labour, though her dilation was still only three fingers wide. Sitt Zakia briskly washed her hands, tested the water temperature and inspected the baby's layette. Only then did she have a seat and catch her breath as she prayed under her breath, 'Bismillah Al-Rahman Al-Raheem.' She asked for a hookah, which was brought within minutes, and then simply waited on the balcony for the labour to progress.

From the mountain, Nablus looked like a burning hearth, its lights aglow like live embers. But there was also darkness, groaning, and the calls of young men. And what about Hussam the fugitive, where was he laying his head tonight? He always arrived with the twittering birds at dawn, at the time of the call to morning prayer. He would tap on the window and say from behind the bars, 'Good morning, Auntie.'

'May your morning be full of joy and your wings soar free! May your day be happy and full of light. Come in, dear boy, come in! Come and rest your eyes.' She would get out of her bed and he would take her place, sleeping till noon.

Once, he came with a friend. They were famished, like a pair of stray cats; they gobbled up all her bread and she had to go and ask the neighbours for some more. A few days later, he came back with the same friend who now had a dumdum bullet lodged in his chest. The young man died in her arms as Hussam sobbed in the dark. Shortly after, he stood out on the flat roof and whistled. A group of young men descended like jinns in the night. They carried him away, burying him in the blink of an eye, without informing his mother. And when Sitt Zakia relayed the terrible news to her, she shrieked as if possessed, 'My only son? Wasn't he also your son? You pulled him out into this world!' And it all came rushing back. God as her witness, she was the one who had cut his umbilical cord and received the congratulations of those surrounding her. She had held him the day of his circumcision and, on that fateful day, had wiped away his final tears. She remembered his cloudy eyes and the tang of his sweat. He died dreaming of a hot bath. They buried him as he was, sweaty, smelling of the stables with wisps of straw caught in his hair.

The cry of the woman in labour yanked her back to reality. She hastened towards her. The tiny head peeped out, then slipped back in, out of sight. The mother fell asleep, her contractions spacing out, slowly receding. Sitt Zakia feared they would stop altogether, so she shouted for the mother to wake up. 'Push! Push! Help your son and push!'

3

She laid out her mattress on the ground, sat down, filled up her hookah and took a few puffs as she listened to it gurgle. Each summer night in Nablus was just like the next: breezes pregnant with the scent of jasmine, dew and whiffs from the sewers. The municipality went to great pains: every morning the marketplace smelt like a freshly cut bouquet of the most fragrant flowers; however, by the time afternoon rolled round—when the hustle and bustle had died down and the shops had closed and the rugs and carts had disappeared along with the cries of the hawkers—the city became a rubbish tip: crumpled papers, plastic bags, used tissues, piles of trampled fruit. Around the hospital, along the high street, on the pavement by the roundabout and near the palm trees, pieces of litter fluttered through the air. The gusts scattered the papers, filled up the plastic bags and lifted the skirts and shawls of the ladies passing by, who would then inevitably put their foot in something soft and brown.

Praise be to God! Glory be to God on His throne, Sitt Zakia thought to herself. *Fog falls on this city like the halo curled around the top of Mount Ebal. Sometimes God blesses us with tender evenings free of worry. No loudspeakers, no calls out into the darkness or cries of Allahu Akbar. No soldiers storming any quarter, near or far. In our city, the near and far blend so well that when we see things from afar, we think that they are close by and when we try to reach them, we discover that they are farther away than Mecca itself. Praise be to God!*

Sitt Zakia had travelled to many a country—Syria, Lebanon, Kuwait, even Saudi Arabia—but she had never seen a city like this one. From the bottom of the valley where she sat along with the rest of those living in the bowels of one of the many alleys of the Bab Al-Saha quarter, she could see it from all sides: the stepped mountains surrounding them, their peaks reaching skywards towards their Creator; and the people moving about like actors on a stage, each playing their role.

But right now, from this hidden flat roof among the domes, the chimney of the bakery and the shingles of the hammam, she was at the height of the minarets and could see the entire quarter without the slightest obstruction blocking her view. Why, there was Um Sadiq the baker, who was still kneading her dough from the afternoon! And there was Um Hamdallah rolling grape leaves and stuffing courgettes, her children sitting around her playing cards. Here was Um Mohammed shaking out a clean quilt atop the pillows of a wooden chaise longue. Who was going to host the young men this evening? Or were people no longer able to host? In this moment the quarter was at its nadir. It seemed that not a day would go by without a new problem rearing its head. No passer-by could escape the harassment of the soldiers occupying Bab Al-Saha: blows, yells, insults and orders of 'Bring paint!' 'Put blanket there!' 'Remove barrier!' and 'Take down flag!' From the top of the roof, Sitt Zakia would see them and invoke God's name. She would hear the beating of her heart and whisper in supplication, 'Your protection on us, O God. Your protection, O All-Knowing One, our guardian.'

Suddenly a whistle went out from the bottom of the alley; a chorus of shrill echoes replied from the mountains. Then gunshots and muzzle sparks of dumdum bullets. Spotlights swept the area. The white mountain was flooded with light. She picked up her hookah, shielding the embers with her hand, and crept away.

4

Samar, the daughter of Um Sadiq the baker, came by in the afternoon with a kilo of a'sabee'—pastries shaped like the fingers of a lady—and a packet of sweet crepes. Sitt Zakia liked Samar and wanted her for her brother's boy, Hussam. Anyone could see that the young girl was pretty, cheerful, a graduate of Al-Najah University and an employee with a salary that was tied to the shekel. If things changed around here, if they calmed down, God willing . . . it might then be possible. Even if Sitt Zakia doubted that such a thing could really happen. In any case, Hussam's mother and father probably wouldn't welcome a baker's daughter with open arms.

Taking a bundle of papers out from her bag, Samar asked, 'Auntie Zakia, I have a survey with me. Can you help me with it?'

The two women sat on a mat by the vines of jasmine, where Hussam had sipped his coffee an hour before. They started to look through the survey.

'How old are you? Married? Divorced? Widowed? What? Not attached or divorced? What does that mean? May God forgive him. Since when? Twenty years? Did you remarry? No? Why?'

'I stayed for my girls.'

'And did he support you financially?'

'We went to court. He was supposed to pay me twenty-five dinars each month. May God forgive him. We went back to the lawyer who said, "Better not make waves, otherwise he'll take the girls!" My brother Abu Azzam helped me out a bit and later on I learnt midwifery and took it from there. At first, I used to go from house to house with Um Ahmad the midwife, then later they accepted me at the hospital and I graduated with a diploma and everything.'

'And your girls? You'd leave them at home alone? And who would cook? Do the grocery shopping? Sweep and dust?'

'Me, myself and I.'

'And how about washing the dishes?'

'The girls. Except a few times when I'd come back at the crack of dawn and find the sink full. I would wash, rinse, cook meals and sit and wait for them to come back from school.'

'Did you ever feel tired? Annoyed? Angry? Ever yell?'

Sitt Zakia clicked her tongue and shook her head.

'So then, never angry? Never got fed up? Never yelled at the girls?'

'I swear to God, I never raised my voice. What good would that do?'

'Then how would you unburden your heavy heart?'

'I'd fill up my hookah and sit on my own, contemplating this world, these mountains, those valleys, and the people below, and the cars up there, driving along, as if they were hanging from invisible threads. At night, when everyone had gone to bed, I'd sit on the roof above the staircase, staring at the stars and moon, breathing in the jasmine and myrtle, celebrating God and all His mercy.'

They exchanged a look full of affection. Sitt Zakia murmured, 'May God keep you happy, how sweet you are! May you be destined for the one I have in mind.'

The young woman's cheeks flushed but she said nothing. Sitt Zakia noticed this and was convinced that Samar had liked what she had proposed. So she tried to get her to talk about it. 'My brother has two sons of marriageable age.'

Samar remained tight-lipped so Sitt Zakia carried on. 'The elder is a doctor, he trained in America. And the younger one, God be praised, will graduate soon and is going to be someone important.'

'You mean Hussam?'

'Yes, Hussam. You know him?'

Samar looked around and stammered, 'I know of him.'

'But do you *know* him?'

Samar nodded her head. Sitt Zakia's heart beat faster.

'And what do you know about him?'

Samar said warmly, 'May God strengthen him and all the other young men. Where would we be without them? I have this feeling that there's going to be another attack soon. Be careful, it's not safe around here.' She looked beyond the edge of the flat rooftop and took in Sakina's house, its shutters still closed. 'There's going to be an attack and we've got to keep our wits about us,' she muttered again.

'It's all the same, we've got nothing to be afraid of.'

Samar shot her a searing look that made Sitt Zakia's blood turn cold. *Your protection, O God! Yes, yes, let us get back to the questionnaire.* 'Are we finished with the survey? Should I make us some coffee?'

Samar let out a yelp of laughter. 'Of course not! Where are you off to? Hold on, and answer this for me: What changes have you seen in women's lives since the Intifada began?'

Sitt Zakia thought for a moment, then whispered, 'You want the truth?'

'Nothing but.'

'Honestly, nothing much has changed for us except more worries. More worrying means more burning hearts. I pray for God to help us women!'

'Auntie Zakia, are you sure about that?' Samar objected. 'Why so pessimistic?'

'What do you want me to say, then? That women have started throwing stones, rescuing the young men, hiding the militants and are out in the streets protesting? Sure. But their misfortune has doubled. Their old worries are still there, and the new ones are too many to count. Pregnancy, weakness, childbirth, breast feeding, laundry, tidying and cleaning, cooking, sighing, nagging from their husbands and children, worrying about the young men roaming out there among the rocks and the wilderness under the blazing summer sun, or in the bitter cold of winter, among the brambles and the howling of wild mountain animals. Worries close to home, worries far away, small worries, big worries, and worrying over the one still in the cot. When he's in your arms, you're afraid he'll be taken. If he's taken, you're afraid he'll be lost. And when they're grown, from the moment he sets foot in prison to when he leaves, you're only running after him from one court to the next, from one door to the next. And if he's not in prison, you'll go searching for him from one cave to the next, from one alley to the next. If you see him you're consumed with worry for him, and if you don't see him you burn for him. Such is our life, worry after worry, from one ordeal to the next. May God help us women.'

Samar protested once more, 'Auntie Zakia, you've forgotten about what our men have to put up with.'

'Oh my dear! We shoulder our worries and *theirs* to boot! They can't keep up with our problems.'

'Now, come on, let's be objective about it.'

'What, my girl? You don't like what I have to say?'

'No, that's not what I meant. Okay, tell me what you want to say.'

'You ask me, then I'll tell you.'

Samar shuffled through her papers, then deliberately asked, 'You . . . as a woman, a midwife, a mother . . . how has the Intifada affected you? Think about it before you answer.'

And think she did. She thought about Hussam, and her girls, married off now, in Kuwait, Saudi Arabia and Oman. Since the beginning of the Intifada she hadn't heard from them, and she probably wouldn't until it ended. But would there really be an end to the Intifada? All this worry, anxiety, blood—was there really an end in sight? She thought of the darkness that she cowered from, the demons and the jinns, the night visits she had to carry out, the abandoned streets and the soldiers harassing her. Nothing scared her like the night, the night and its darkness, the army raids, sudden skirmishes and those wounded by stray bullets. Worse than all this, though, was the fear that she felt but didn't dare express: sometimes she found herself right in the thick of it with nowhere to run or hide. Her simple tools would become surgical ones. She would stitch this up, set the splint for that, extract a bullet or administer an injection. She was the nurse and the midwife, the bearer of good news and bad, the dove and the owl. She would make her way from house to house— at some, announcing the best of news; at others, the worst: Your son has been injured. Your son died a martyr. God help your son, dear woman. Where's my gift for the safe delivery?

'So, Auntie Zakia, what do you have to say?'

'About?'

'How has the Intifada affected you as a woman, midwife and mother?'

'My worries are endless, my heart aches, and I've seen things that I never dreamt I'd see in my lifetime.'

'Be more precise, Auntie, more precise.'

'What do you want me to be more precise about, my girl? There are certain things I can't even say, let alone be more precise about.'

'Okay then, tell me about your work. Has your work been affected by the Intifada?'

'Leave that aside. Only God knows. This is war! A lot of things change, but always for the worse . . . '

Samar cut her off, 'No, not necessarily.'

'Just listen to me.' Sitt Zakia lowered her voice, slid next to Samar and looked in the direction of Sakina's house. The windows and shutters were closed. 'You see that house over there?'

'You mean Sakina's house?

'Shush, keep your voice down.'

'What about that house?' Samar whispered.

'Do you know what goes on there?'

'I know.'

'Do you know why?'

'I'm not sure. When conducting scientific research, you've always got to be exact about things, completely sure.'

'Oh, this scientific research of yours! What research? And how can we be exact and completely sure? The best we can do is guess.'

'We've got to be completely sure.'

'May God protect you, my girl. The only person who could give us hard facts has left for good, and her case is closed.'

'They say that her son has joined the young men.'

'Yes, that's what they say.'

'They also say that Nuzha is innocent, wrongly accused, and it's unfair for her to go through what she has.'

'Yes, they say that too.'

'Others say that she collaborated with the Israelis, that she's a good-for-nothing, and that she's just like her mother.'

'Yes, they also say that.'

'But how can we be exact and completely sure?'

'My dear, I already told you, the best we can do is guess.'

'But with scientific research . . . '

'What scientific research? Who's free to conduct such research? It's already difficult enough to find our way around at night. Wallah, I tell you, when I'm walking, my hands are outstretched in front of me like a blind bat. Maybe it's the end of the world and Judgement Day is approaching, "The day where man flees from his brother, his friend and his children," as the Quran says.'

'What's all this talk, Auntie?'

'Two brothers, born of the same mother, from the same womb. One is a masked man fighting for his country and the other is a traitor. How is that possible? Tell me!'

'*You* tell me.'

'Because it's the end of the world and Judgement Day approaches.'

'What are you talking about?'

'Just listen to me. They say Sakina might have been killed by her own son.'

'You just said, "might have ..."'

'Only God knows, but that's what they say.'

'Okay, and Nuzha?'

'What about her?'

'How do we know if she's innocent or not?'

'But what can we do, my girl?'

'We must do something.'

'Like what?'

'Like, if she's innocent, we should reach out and help her.'

Sitt Zakia's face blanched with fright. 'Goodness, anything but that!'

'Wasn't it you, Sitt Zakia, who pulled her out of her mother's womb?'

'With my own two hands.'

'So you're like a mother to her.'

'There is no strength ...'

'Suppose she's been wrongly accused.'

'And if she has?'

'We've got to help her, Hajja!'

'And how can we do that? We can hardly help ourselves.'

Samar lowered her neck and muttered, 'And they call you Mama!'

Sitt Zakia spoke up in her defence. 'What can I do with my bare hands? Tell me. And you, and your association, what can you do? Tell me!'

'Me? I'm going to go meet her and get her to fill in my survey.'

'No! Don't you dare. Don't be a fool!' exclaimed Sitt Zakia in fear.

Samar gathered up her papers, kissed Sitt Zakia and whispered, 'Whatever you say, or however scared you are, you'll always be Mama to us.'

5

That time with Samar was the first time that she had allowed herself to let down her guard and relax a little. Everyone knew that Sitt Zakia was usually taciturn, discreet and didn't carry secrets from one house to another. Whenever she found herself at get-togethers where the women gathered round the hookahs and cups of coffee, gossiping about their husbands and attacking the reputation of others, she would always remain silent, unmoving. She was certain that the women respected her approach to things and welcomed her discretion. By harbouring the secret of one house, and remaining unforthcoming about another's, she was guarding all of their secrets, veiling what she saw in each house. Even though they mocked her at these gatherings for not joining in their mud-slinging, complaining and scandal-mongering, she knew that one wrong step, one slip of the tongue would be the end of her career and her status as 'Mama', would shatter her reputation as a pillar of the community.

She shook her head and smiled ruefully as she took in the women jabbering away, grumbling about this or that. She so yearned to be like them: to open her mouth once and never have to close it. To let it run wild, yell, curse her husband and her misfortune, curse the night and the jinns and demons that it harboured . . . but she never did so. She wasn't used to it or, rather, she had worked hard to not get used to such a luxury, accepting her lot as a mere listener.

'What a vault you are Sitt Zakia!' Um Sadiq the baker remarked, 'Never once in your life have you poured your heart out to us or revealed your secrets, while we share everything with you and hold you so dear.'

The two other neighbours, Um Hamdallah and Um Mohammed guffawed while passing the hookah beak back and forth between them. Um Mohammed, who was not known for her discretion, said, 'Would it be right for a woman as sharp as Sitt Zakia to speak her mind in the presence of two of the loosest tongues in the quarter?'

Um Hamdallah gasped and beat her chest, 'Goodness, look who's speaking now. After what happened to Sakina, you shouldn't be talking at all, not even half a word.'

Um Mohammed smiled at this accusation, considering it a medal confirming what she was capable of. 'And what do I have to do with Sakina?'

'Who was it that revealed what she had been up to and got her killed?'

Such an accusation was no longer a laughing matter. Um Mohammed's face tightened. 'Again, what do I have to do with it? Weren't *you* the ones who said that she's a traitor, a madam, that her home was a brothel for Jews? Aren't you the one who said as much, Um Sadiq?'

'Me? *Me*?!' squawked Um Sadiq. 'Say something, Sitt Zakia! By the life of the Prophet, say something!'

Sitt Zakia said nothing but just sat smiling. Yes, Um Sadiq had said such things, as had Um Mohammed and Um Hamdallah. They all had, really, except for Samar. She alone had asked her bizarre question, 'How can we be exact and completely sure?'

'Okay,' Sitt Zakia calmly interjected, 'How about we leave those poisonous tales alone. Come on, take a puff.' She held out the folded pipe and Um Hamdallah took it, sucking in so strongly that the embers crackled, then passed it on to Um

Sadiq. After a few minutes Um Mohammed whispered, 'Have you all seen what those young men did to Nuzha?' Sitt Zakia remained silent. Um Sadiq and Um Mohammed's eyes grew as big as saucers, impatient. 'They jumped from rooftop to rooftop, until they reached her garden and told her, "Look here, Nuzha, either you listen to us and we forgive you and forget your past, or, if you insist on being like your mother, what happened to her will happen to you."'

'And after that?' urged Um Sadiq.

'There was no before and after. You think she could have said no to them?'

'She could have said yes but then done the opposite,' Um Sadiq said from experience.

'What does that mean?'

'That a dog's tail will always be bent, no matter how many times you set it straight.'

'You shouldn't say such things, my dear,' Um Hamdallah said sadly.

'It's neither good nor bad. Like mother, like daughter. Can a thorn birth a rose?'

Sitt Zakia pondered on the question and replied, 'Who knows!'

But Um Sadiq wouldn't drop it. 'So Sitt Zakia, do you think that a young girl, beautiful and shameless, can settle down one day?' No one responded. Only the gurgling of the hookah pierced the silence. After a long moment, Sitt Zakia asked herself pensively, 'Well then, Um Mohammed, tell me this, where did you hear all this that you're going on about? How do you know about it, and how can you be completely sure about it all?'

'Soon, all of you will hear about it. You'll find out it's true, and remember that I'm the one who told you in the first place,' Um Mohammed boasted.

6

It was in fact the very next day that Sitt Zakia found out for herself that it was true. She was shuffling home at dawn, exhausted from helping out with a difficult delivery. The alleyways were still quiet. Some of the grocers were emptying their crates and arranging their fruit and vegetables into small pyramids. The bean and chickpea sellers were still stirring their broth. In the middle of the lane where Sakina's house sat, a window opened and Nuzha appeared, her head unusually covered with a shawl. She looked to the right, then to the left and whispered, 'Sitt Zakia, can I have a word?'

Sitt Zakia stood frozen under the window. She was worn out, light-headed, eyelids drooping, sapped of the strength to shoulder any more burdens. And of all places, this house was the root of so many problems. Sitt Zakia already had more than her fair share of those.

'For God's sake, I beg you! Help me,' insisted Nuzha, becoming more hysterical with each passing second.

Help her? She wasn't like that young thing Samar to have such ideas and naive plans. In such dark days, it was difficult for people to even help themselves!

'I'm begging you, Sitt Zakia.'

Sitt Zakia leant against the wall, adjusted her yanis—her lengthy headscarf covering her bosom—wiped her face and called upon God for strength, power and His divine mercy. Having pity on Nuzha, she raised her head. 'Come upstairs, just for a moment, and I'll tell you,' she heard Nuzha urge her.

Anything but that! To enter this den of scandal and calamity? My God, completely out of the question, not even if someone put the world in her right hand and the sun in her left.

'Auntie Zakia . . . '

'I'm not your auntie . . . I'm not coming in means just that, I'm not coming in.'

'In the name of the prophet, please come in.'

'Just tell me what you have to say, and let me be on my way. I didn't sleep a wink the whole night,' Sitt Zakia grumbled.

She raised her head and her gaze met two eyes that could only be described by praising the Most High. *Praise be to the Creator on His throne! Your face, O God, is glorified, splendid and luminous, O Most Merciful.*

'Hold on, I'm coming down,' Nuzha said quickly. In a matter of moments, Sitt Zakia heard the iron gate creak and the rustle of the young woman's footsteps on the stairs. Then there she was, slender, alabaster white. How was she so white? And those ice-blue eyes! Her melodic voice! It wouldn't surprise her if she could also play the oud!

'You won't come in?'

'No,' Sitt Zakia said, shaking her head decisively.

Nuzha's head drooped, dejected. Sitt Zakia's heart went out to her and she nearly gave in. But she was jolted by the sudden change in Nuzha's features, her face becoming taut, like a mask of plaster of Paris.

'H-Hussam,' she stuttered, her voice hoarse.

'What about Hussam?'

Nuzha didn't respond, she just kept repeating, 'Hussam. Hussam.'

Anxiety gripped Sitt Zakia. 'What about him?' When the girl still didn't say anything, she grabbed her dress sleeve. 'What about Hussam? Speak! Tell me!'

But Nuzha remained silent. She simply kept staring at Sitt Zakia, her eyebrow raised, her eyes insolent.

The old woman nearly broke down. 'Have they found him? Arrested him? Who would have given him up? After what happened to you and your mother, is it possible that . . . ?' She shook Nuzha by the shoulders. 'Tell me! Speak!'

Nuzha stumbled a few steps back, as she kept repeating, 'It's him all right, it's him.' She kept backing away and disappeared into the darkness at the top of the stairs. Unaware of what she was doing, and against her will, Sitt Zakia cast her reservations to the wind and followed Nuzha. She climbed up the dark, narrow, twisting staircase, her knees knocking against each other. When she reached the final step, Nuzha pulled her inside and swiftly shut the door behind them. She dragged Sitt Zakia by the hand to the middle of the sitting room and made her sit on the velvet sofa by the shelves. Sitt Zakia rested her head on the edge of the sofa and began to gasp for air, short of breath. Through the fog clouding her mind, she heard, 'Sitt Zakia, forgive me, I lied to you.'

She turned to the voice and was once more surprised by the quick change in Nuzha's face, tears freely running down her cheeks. She wept dejectedly. 'I only said Hussam was here so that you'd come in,' she confessed.

Sitt Zakia didn't comment. She turned her face away, overcome by fear and revulsion.

Suddenly the young girl began to shriek, 'Look!' Nuzha pulled at her headscarf, revealing the side of her face, her neck, all the while shrieking. 'Look! Look!' Sitt Zakia took in red splotches and blue-black contusions. She held her breath and asked for God's forgiveness. In a heartbeat, Nuzha had slipped down from the sofa and crashed to the ground, tugging at Sitt Zakia's legs, yelping, making the strangest of sounds. Even those who have been renounced, hopeless widows and the devastated mothers of newly made martyrs didn't make sounds like this. Without knowing what she was doing, Sitt Zakia found herself leaning over her and saying, 'Get up my girl, get up. God is always greater.'

7

While Nuzha went to prepare some tea, Sitt Zakia's eyes roamed over every nook and cranny of the house. It was the first time in twenty years that she'd set foot inside Sakina's house, maybe even since Nuzha's birth—when Sakina had still been seen as an honourable woman. It was an ancient house, which dated back to before the earthquake of 1927, and had belonged to a family of high standing, one known for manufacturing soap and detergent. When wealthy families started leaving the old city for the suburbs and mountains, the house became deserted and remained as such until its walls cracked and its wooden window frames were on the verge of falling apart. Then one day, a man from an unknown family who had worked in one of the Gulf countries bought it and set about restoring the walls, pruning the branches of the lemon tree, painting the ceilings with anti-mould paint and installing solar panels.

At first, as usual, the quarter welcomed these new neighbours with questions and rumours. The man was old but his wife was young; he was ill but she was fit as a fiddle, pretty, sharp, with baby-blue eyes. People stopped gossiping when there was nothing juicy left to comment on. She was a respectable woman, modest, discreet. She never visited anyone and no one ever called on her. Her children were no different from the rest of those running around the neighbourhood, except for their blue eyes and blonde hair.

The house became a paradise of orderliness and cleanliness. During the day, the wife would be seen hanging out of the towering windows, rubbing the panes and shining them till they sparkled like diamonds. As for the stone stairs leading to the garden, which were hidden behind the house and which no one could see except from the highest of windows, they were shimmering white. Her children were always the paragon of health, their cheeks flushing pink.

The husband was in his late fifties while his wife was still in her twenties. While he grew hunchbacked and then eventually died, she remained young and attractive and her children gleamed like pieces of the moon itself.

Soon after his demise, the house began to fall back into its dilapidated state. The lemon tree's branches became overgrown, weeds overran the garden and the solar panels cracked. The lady of the house stopped tidying up, washing up or polishing the panes, and spent her time sewing and embroidering instead. One day, the sound of the oud was heard, and the chatter of foreign voices and accents followed by strange smells. The rumour mill went into overdrive.

'God's protection upon us! Is this what Nablus has come to? What about our daughters? And the quarter, our square, the reputation of our streets is at stake! By God, we must act and spit blood upon this whore!' But no one lifted a finger. The unknown faces kept coming, ever watchful, with eyes peeled and ears pricked. And there were dollars and shekels, of course.

The house sparkled once more, the windowpanes gleaming and its steps radiant. But the smell of soap in the air was different. Not only that, but the number of solar panels multiplied, the number of hanging towels swelled, the branches of the garden were lit up by fairy lights and loudspeakers pulsed to the beat of foreign music.

The rumours lost their momentum, not because the house and what happened inside had changed at all but, rather, because it wasn't the only one of its kind in the city or even in the quarter. All types of strange smells bombarded the city. All springs flowed, except the natural ones. A strange stupor overcame the inhabitants of the area.

Then the Intifada came and the city was jolted awake. Fear began to fall like yellowing autumn leaves. The mountains, vineyards and valleys flared up. People came out onto the streets and the hashish traders soon went bankrupt. Spies went underground but the knives of the young men flushed them out. The stone square known as Bab Al-Saha became a slaughterhouse where collaborators were strung from hooks like mutton. It was newly christened Al-Saha Al-Hamraa, the

Scarlet Square. And it was there, on the steps of the mosque in the heart of this square, that Sakina was found, a dagger plunged into her chest.

Nuzha came back with a tray of tea. Out of habit, she stopped in front of mirror of the old engraved wooden bureau, inlaid with mother of pearl. In this decor of velvet, mother of pearl and crystal, she looked like a statue sculpted from marble.

'Praise be to the Creator on His throne!' mumbled Sitt Zakia in admiration, in spite of herself. Nuzha advanced towards her, babbling. As soon as she set the tray down on the table, she fell down once more at Sitt Zakia's feet, tugging her legs to her chest as she pled, 'Just let me see him, for God's sake, just let me see him.'

8

When she returned home, she found Hussam fast asleep in her bed. She left him there and lay out on the wooden chaise longue till the next morning. She woke up to the aroma of coffee. Upon opening her eyes she saw him sitting by the jasmine vines, shielded from the neighbours' prying eyes. She looked at him for some time, trying to come to a decision. He looked so much younger than he actually was. He could still be mistaken for a teenager even though he had crossed that bridge long ago.

He turned to her and saw her taking him in. His grin disarmed her and melted her heart. She wondered to herself, could he really be one of *them*? His face as smooth as a young girl's, his half-open eyes, his quiet voice. Could he really be what they say he is? But he fears God, believes in Him. He wouldn't hurt a fly. Would he?

'Coffee?' he asked, holding up the steaming pot. The heady aroma of coffee beans and cloves laced with jasmine filled her head, making her dizzy and melancholy all at once. She wiped away delicate tears all the while praising God.

He smiled again and asked her, 'Girl or boy?'

'Girl,' she mumbled absentmindedly.

'So you didn't get a gift for the good news,' he teased her.

'A girl! It was a girl. What do you want me to do?'

'Oh Auntie, as if having a girl is a calamity,' he chuckled.

She shook her head distractedly and kept sipping her coffee in silence.

He tried to provoke her, 'When I marry, I'll only have girls.'

'You know our family only ever has boys.'

He laughed once more. 'But you were different.'

'Me? So you want to get married to be like me and have girls? The burden of a daughter is till the day you die.' Nuzha's face, branded by humiliation and fear, came to mind. She repeated, 'The burden of a daughter is till the day you die.'

He stared at her silently, then anxiously asked, 'What's wrong? You're not your self. Is everything okay?'

For the first time, she met his eyes. 'It's Nuzha, Sakina's girl.'

He turned his face away and blinked hard but didn't utter a word.

'She wants to see you. She got down on her knees and kissed my hands, begging me. She wants to see you.'

He stayed silent as if she had spoken to someone else altogether.

'So, what do you think?' Sitt Zakia urged him.

Looking off into the distance he wondered aloud, 'What do *you* think?'

'What on earth could I say! Wallah, I don't know anything. What could I know?'

Still far away, he added, 'When you know, tell me.' Moments later he turned to her, stared at her and insisted, 'What would you do if you were in my shoes?' She didn't respond, so he threw out his bait, 'If you tell me to go see her, I'll go.'

'No, don't you dare!'

The corners of his mouth turned upwards. 'So then?'

'I don't know anything. She begged me and I . . . I'm just the messenger.'

'Still, tell me what you think.'

'I wouldn't know where to start. I don't know anything.'

She recalled the sobbing face and the hands that had gripped her. She recalled the smooth touch of Nuzha's hair and her back shuddering beneath her palms. She recalled how her mind refused to compare Nuzha to her own daughters. She had been about to leave when Nuzha had asked her to 'Think of me as one of your own girls.' Sitt Zakia had then wrenched her hand free, horrified, shooting her a cruel look. Nuzha broke down sobbing, throwing her head on the old lady's shoulder. 'Please, I beg you, let me see him.'

Taken aback, Sitt Zakia responded to her nephew, 'So you would listen to what she has to say?'

'We've heard all that she has to say,' he said resolutely, in a clipped tone she wasn't familiar with. The words buzzed round in her head. *We've heard, we've heard. You've heard? You and who else? You and they? They, who jumped from roof to roof to rough her up? They, who plunged the knife into her mother's chest, so deep only the hilt was visible? Are you one of them?* She didn't dare utter her question aloud. She was terrified of hearing the word 'Yes'. What if he did say 'Yes'? If he raised his hand and declared, 'I'm the one who both judges and condemns, with this very hand here.' She turned her attention back to him.

He kept on insisting, 'If you tell me to go, I'll go over there right now.'

She didn't say anything but let herself get lost in her thoughts: *The burden of a daughter is till the day you die.*

9

Hussam belonged to that group of people who felt everything. They believed—perhaps due to their privileged circumstances—that they were responsible for changing the way things were. He wasn't one of the tent dwellers, or one of those who had been abused by the streets, or a beggar in the ravines or the mountains. He was a man whose life had started out mediocrely and continued as such in every aspect. He was from a family that was mediocrely rich, educated to a mediocre standard, mediocre in their claims to nobility and prestige. His uncles, on the other hand, were anything but mediocre. They had migrated to Kuwait, Saudi Arabia and Germany, becoming so filthy rich that they were indifferent to what they inherited from their father: the remains of a house destroyed by the earthquake in the middle of town next to Bab Al-Saha; an oil press; and an isolated vineyard on the borders of a nearby village. Due to the winds of progress and urbanization, the vineyard bought by their grandfather for the price of a morsel of bread was now worth a great fortune, even though it remained untilled. The situation of the country at that time had made it difficult for their father to sell; people were afraid of selling and dreaded buying. When they did buy though, it was one plot here, another one there, just enough for building a house or a handful of boutiques.

Mr Wajih, dubbed Abu Azzam, had sold two lots on the main road and kept the rest of the land for himself, on which he built a sprawling villa, giving the impression he was more of a somebody than he actually was. Propelled by visions of grandeur—of riches and prestige that had seized his peers ever since the spurting of oil in far-off countries other than their own—he was wholly convinced that he, too, deserved to be in the higher echelons of society. How could he not be, when he had all the trappings of a noble man? Take his wife for instance, who was from a respectable family; his brothers—either doctors, functionaries or expert advisors who played the currency game; his children, who were advancing along the same path that their uncles had trod, with the same ambition; and finally his villa with more red tiles and glass panes than that of someone with a bigger bank balance or higher up on the societal ladder.

Only two things stained his past and his present: his half-sister, the midwife who lived in a rundown alley, next to Bab Al-Saha; his son, the runt of the litter, bursting with these ideas that poisoned everyone's lives and hindered his journey towards assured success. What was it actually that was stopping that boy from being the apple of his father's eye? He was eloquent, handsome and pleasant, loved a good discussion and devoured books.

But he was mercurial, sometimes acting like someone who had been touched in the head. He was always swimming against the tide. Every time his father told him to do something, he did the opposite. He would do anything but that which he was asked to do. Abu Azzam said, study engineering or medicine; his son chose philosophy and history. He suggested that he study abroad, knowing that foreign diplomas were more highly valued; his son opted to attend Al-Najah University instead. After his son's first brush with the law, he recommended that he go to America or London. After all, Abu Azzam had a plot of land that he could sell and transfer the money into an account abroad for him. 'You'd do better to transfer it to my uncles—it's their right to have it after all. Or compensate your sister for what's actually hers,' his son spat back.

It was during that night that he had his so-called heart attack. Not only was his brothers' right to the land nagging at him, but, after all this time, Zakia's portion as well. In fact, her portion hadn't been eaten up . . . not completely, that is. Because there was what he had given her when her husband, that vile piece of work, had left her. If it weren't for him she would have died of hunger. But how quickly people forget!

To tell the truth, Zakia was different, not like other women. When Hussam had spurred her to reclaim her rightful portion, she had responded with righteous indignation, 'Shame on you for saying such things! It's not right for a sister to cross her brother.' Surprised by her response, Hussam asked her to elaborate. Finding herself unable to do so, she simply repeated, 'Tsk! How shameful!' But this didn't prevent her brother Abu Azzam from having his little heart attack, which at the time the doctor didn't even diagnose as a heart attack, and yet he insisted upon bed rest for some days, days where he only slurped soup, sipped orange juice and swallowed milk.

Abu Azzam was stingy, even though his villa suggested otherwise: marble flooring, ceiling decor, elaborate wallpaper and works of art directly imported from Rome. But when it came to buying the daily needs for the house, how he would swing to the other end of the spectrum! He would choose the absolute worst of what was on offer in the market. Cucumbers as shapeless as potatoes, flabby aubergines that seemed to have already been cooked, courgettes with seeds as hard as a pumpkin's, stringy radishes as soft as a worn-out sponge.

Poor Um Azzam, she who couldn't buy anything, not even a bunch of parsley. Everyone knew that he had sworn to divorce her if he found out that she had gone out as far as the roundabout, or walked in the marketplace or the old city. When she wanted to buy a pair of socks, she would have to perform a complicated series of steps, the first of which was to wait until her husband's stormy mood broke, allowing for some sun to peek through the clouds. Then she'd have to murmur in a tone as humble as a prayer, 'Abu Azzam, may God protect you, a pair of socks, please.'

His bushy caterpillar eyebrows would arch as he exclaimed in surprise, 'Socks? Where did all your socks go?'

She would hasten to flatter him, 'May you live long and always be blessed!'

'Yes, God willing.' His bulging, buggy eyes would lock onto her. 'What happened to all your socks?'

'Finished,' she would respond fearfully. 'They're completely melted.'

He would stare at her, searing straight through her flesh. 'Melted?' Then he would drum his nails on the tabletop. 'Melted, you say.' His mouth would crack open, flashing his yellow teeth. 'Melted, melted,' he would repeat, his voice rising to a crescendo, 'But how?'

The sheer boom of his voice would make her backtrack in alarm. 'Forget it, I didn't say anything.'

Then he would take his aim, 'Forget about it? You didn't say anything? First, explain how they melted. Sugar, yes, that melts. And salt too. But *socks*? Tell me first how they melted.'

Looking frantically from side to side, she would splutter, 'It's not important.'

'Aha! It's not important. What are you trying to say? Have I ever denied you anything? Tell me first, how did they melt?'

She would scamper off, avoiding him for the rest of the evening. He too would also ignore her, not breathing a word to her, nor sleeping next to her that night. Sometimes if she had asked for something bigger, bigger than a pair of socks, the punishment would last even longer: a day, two days, a month, maybe more. During those times, Um Azzam would feel that her days with him were numbered, that he was preparing to divorce her or take a second wife. In those moments, the poor woman would become like the shuttle of a sewing machine: she would pace to one side of the room, then to the other, go up the stairs, then down, never sitting still, except when she gave in to sleep. She would become like an old dog, trailing him everywhere, even to the bathroom. She would attend to his every need, even the most personal: cutting his toenails, trimming his ear hair, snipping his armpit hair, squeezing blackheads out from his nose and laughing at even his crassest remarks.

After all this mollycoddling, he would be in high spirits. So after a week or two he would give her the socks and she would be over the moon, almost crying in gratitude, and would go back to ardently singing his praises.

She would look intently at his bulging eyes, and then behind him, at the wallpaper, black marble, the crystal, and say to herself, 'This palace is mine, the car, the olive grove, this garage, this trellis, this tile roof, these vines, the grapes, the hedge and the iron gate, praise be to God.' But on those depressed evenings when she watched *Vincent*, a TV show inspired by *Beauty and the Beast*, and saw the beast's wild face with his heart of gold, crawling out of the gutters to meet his beloved and recite her a sonnet, she would cry silently and wish with her whole being that she lived in the gutter.

10

Wajih was fiercely proud of his children, so much so that he couldn't love them. At least that is the impression that Hussam had. He would collect them like a miser collects pieces of gold, hiding them away in a tightly sealed box far from his reach and out of sight, never touching them except to count them. It was enough for him to simply delight in the knowledge that he had such an enviable fortune that he could rely on when necessary. Hussam couldn't remember a single day when his father had spoilt him or spoken to him openly, from the heart. He wasn't the only one; his brothers suffered the same fate. As soon as he returned home, the children would line up along the stairs like little soldiers, from the eldest on the highest step to the youngest. Hussam of course was at the bottom. 'Good evening, Yaba,' the eldest would say fearfully. Hussam would feel just as uneasy.

His mother would be at the entrance, by the large house-plant with mammoth leaves stacked like a ribcage. The uglier the scene, the better the outcome. Hussam sought refuge in the room by the roof where a jumble of objects was piled up: old pieces of furniture, dusty lanterns without bulbs, his grandmother's trousseau and leftover Chinese tiles from when the house had been built. He would sit there, as if guarding a sacred temple, listening to the copper trinkets of an old hanging lamp clinking away as they swayed in the breeze. It was here that he would read books borrowed from the municipal library and see the image of his beloved on every page.

When he met her for the first time, he felt a tremor travel through his body. An electric shock set his heart alight, the flames spreading to his head. Tears fell from his eyes for no reason, uncontrollable—he wasn't sad, in pain or even afraid. But pour down they did just the same.

She was older, a teacher at the school with the wide steps, and he, well he had been young. So he had tried to grow up.

He had been sitting on the green bench in the park of the municipal library, in the midst of the cypresses, poppies, countless sparrow's nests, chirping and the rustle of the leaves in the wind. It was a damp, windy autumn day. Her skirt had ballooned like the sail of a parting ship, revealing her hidden thighs and even higher up than that. She brought down her arms as quickly as she could and pulled at the sides, while the wind continued to tease her. She turned this way and that, trying to escape the gust, and he saw her from another angle, remaining speechless, his mouth agape. She saw him looking thunderstruck. She opened her eyes— sparkling white—wide and smiled. An electric current coursed through his entire being. Tears started flowing again so he was forced to turn his face away. Bitterly he thought, *But why did she smile? If I were older she wouldn't have smiled.* And from that day he had his first taste of sleepless nights, burning with longing.

He started to follow her like a madman. Every day he would go to the library: read, dream, mope, doze off, pick up where he left off and then plunge once more into his thoughts. Days went by and he didn't see her. Then suddenly she appeared. Without any forewarning. Mostly she would come after school had let out in the afternoon. He would observe her from behind the glass, swaying in her high heels, fashionably dressed. She was as slender as bamboo, some days in tight skirts moulded to her hips and on others in airy skirts or a summer blazer giving her a sophisticated sporty look. She would linger at the counter to return books and then let herself get lost between the shelves, her heels clacking on the floor tiles.

He started to do some digging: her name, degree, where she graduated from, her father's name and that of her family. Her father was an honest carpenter while her brothers were still young. She was the eldest. She had studied biology and graduated from the American University of Beirut after getting a scholarship for being in the top ten. So she was intelligent and of sound mind! AUB and biology? Good God! He might as well read all the books on earth!

What did she read? Literature, philosophy, politics, science, history, more politics, economics, political poetry, politics and more politics. So then what was he waiting for to read all of this and that, so that he could listen, discuss and be political?

Now that he was remembering the seed of politics in his far-off past, he made a dangerous confession, that if it hadn't been for her, he wouldn't have dived into politics as deeply as he did. Like everyone else, he had only been floating on the surface: following events, the Occupation, growing poverty and waiting for a revolution that would come from the other side through Jordan.

He had grown considerably older when he heard her voice for the first time. For more than two years he had been chasing her in his dreams, in his borrowed books and the library. He had graduated from secondary school and applied to Al-Najah University. It was then that he had been arrested by chance, put into administrative detention, a rite of passage for all young men, after which he conquered his fears. He was no longer afraid of his overbearing father. He no longer stood in a line on the stairs and said meekly, 'Good evening, Yaba.' He no longer feared looking girls straight in the eyes. He no longer felt that looking was a sort of betrayal. But more important than all this, he was no longer convinced of this love, this one-sided love, this love of his dreams, which came from the pages of books and a desire buried in the depths of his soul. A lucid mind is a sure thing, he would tell himself. His readings began to bear fruit. Now he understood what he was reading; he could analyse, justify and meditate on meanings. He started visiting the room by the roof less and less, amid the piles of junk and the chiming of the clocks. He started to frequent Bab Al-Saha more, and Khan Al-Tujjar. He joined his first organization and was arrested and detained for three months. After university he joined the ranks of a second group, then prison again for a year and a half. By the time he was released, he had hardened and gained a deeper understanding of how things worked. He knew what he wanted, and he always wanted to know more.

The next time he saw her was at a book fair. Still just as chic, wrapped-up, in her high heels. She was still but a dream for him; he felt his heart beat slowly and yet ill at ease as ever. He approached the table where she stood turning over a new book. In a defiant tone, he said, 'What a country this is! It's been five years or more and still I know you without really knowing you.'

She turned round swiftly and was forced to look up to him. He had shot up, taller than her! Their eyes met. She slowly whispered in a rich, husky voice, 'You're not tearing up!'

'I've grown,' he said with calculated coolness.

'Clearly,' she said, nodding her head.

How had he let himself get so carried away? It was his first love, rather his first and his last. In this love, tenderness blurred with sparks of the head and shivers of the body. The sun shone more brightly, the earth was richer and the old city seemed a mirage. He walked now in the Kasbah quarter, roaming between the old buildings, arches and wide rosemary hedges. He inhaled the aromas of sesame oil, hot pepper, freshly baked bread, shish kebab, black cumin, sumac, mana'eesh flatbread topped with za'tar, the hot sweet cinnamon drink kinar, tahini halva and nutmeg-topped deserts. In these cloth sacks were spices of the world. He caught glimpses of light slipping through the openings and took in the gilded stars of the mosque, the ceiling of the market and the cupolas.

Now, Hussam no longer felt the same thrill rebelling against his father. As soon as he saw his car back out, he would hop over the fence and go inside to sit in front of one of the bay windows, stretch out his legs and daydream. The autumn sun would filter through the glass, bringing with it the warmth and luminosity of the world.

How does this city get all this coruscating light? And what about this expanse of horizon from the west till the sea mist? At far-off evening, the sun fades away, becoming a breeze that loosens up one's joints. On the roof of the house, Hussam sat drunk with happiness, inhaling the perfumed air, the smell of the earth, dreaming of reaching the furthest point: that of immortality, an extreme languor of the soul and an all-encompassing love for every being.

The hills of Zawata, Mount Rubeen, the broad valleys which sloped to welcome the sun and the love of a girl whose eyes were the wings of dusk, the plumage of a swallow and golden ears of grain. Woman was and still is an image, a symbol of the land. Or maybe it's the land that *is* the woman. But land was no longer for him the dream of all dreams. Now, having paid the heavy price, he knew how someone could die on a rock or in a deserted den like a jackal. And if he hadn't had faith, believing from his heart, he would have shut everything and even everyone out. But for him, people were the temple, the Kaaba, the focal point of every prayer. Without them, what would the earth taste like? What would the taste of the soul and the meaning of nationhood be?

He still remembered Samih's dreams. Both had been sitting on the edge of a rock, far from the balconies of the city. Samih had said with great conviction, 'Tomorrow when there's a state and peace comes, I'll build a home here, all its sides of glass. You know why? I don't want to miss a single bit of this shimmering beauty.'

'You're such a poet!' exclaimed Hussam.

Samih turned to him and smiled wanly. 'Me? A poet? What are you going on about? I can hardly read or write. A sewage worker is what I am. Gutters are what I know, nothing else.'

'Do you think that poetry is a science? Weren't there poets before Islam? And what about the Bedouin and gypsy poets? How about the singers at celebrations and weddings? I have an aunt, she's a midwife but she's more poetic than the great Antar himself.'

'Really? A midwife, you say?'

'A midwife in Bab Al-Saha. But when she sits amid the domes and breathes in the smell of tobacco, she gets high on it, soars up above, all of her words becoming images. We'll slip in one day and I'll take you to her.'

He took him to her a first time and then a second. That was the last time. Tears pricked his eyes. Sometimes when he lets down his guard and meditates, he loses his mind and becomes like an injured animal. *What did we gain? What did we lose? Where were we then, and where are we now? How far will we go? Is there an end, a hope in sight? Stop it, all this rambling, these mind games! The poisonous doubt creeping in, your mind wandering, loneliness, we don't have time for such luxuries. Run! Hide! Punch! Warn them! Call out! Whistle! Give orders! Make a plan! Pass messages! Bury him! Dig! Carry this! Then suffer, put up with, laugh, and laugh some more at the height of your grief. You are the builder and the destroyer, the world and the immortality of the earth.*

II

He woke up to the noise of a suspicious clatter. Two cats were meowing, fighting in the garden of Sakina's house. From the upstairs window, the night was as black as kohl. Suddenly the phone rang but his aunt didn't pick it up. It kept on ringing and ringing while he looked out of the window. After she had finally responded, he heard her footsteps approaching. When he turned to face her, she was leaning against the door.

'That was Samar telling us to get up.'

Silently, he observed her black silhouette in the ring of dim light.

'She has never called at this late an hour in her life!' she remarked, wringing her hands.

He went back to looking out the window and saw shadows creeping along the wall, clinging to it. 'They've attacked the quarter. I've got to go,' he said in a detached voice.

She put her arm out to block him. 'No, don't you dare. If they see you, they'll shoot you. Come with me.' She walked in front of him, a flashlight in hand. Slowly, they went down the stairs until they reached the ground floor. She opened the window leading to the manwar—the narrow, vertical light shaft—and said, 'Go through there, the hill's just through there.'

She closed the window behind him.

He looked up and saw the stars at the top of the shaft, and then light beams dancing behind Um Sadiq's windows. Moments later her upstairs window opened and he heard her children whispering to each other, 'Yallah, move it.' He flattened himself against the wall and let out a 'Shush!'

The figure in the window froze. 'Who's there?'

'Hussam.'

'Hurry up!' The first jumped down the shaft, then a second, and then a third. Um Hamdallah's window opened and two figures leapt out; one more emerged from Um Mohammed's.

In the darkness one of them said, 'It's going to be cramped in there. Get ready, you lot!'

'You think it's wide enough?' a confused voice piped up.

'It'll do, it'll do, just be ready!'

The attack began. Searchlights suddenly flickered to life, then the night burnt neon orange. 'Squeeze in!' the order came. Hussam's body was squashed against others. A thought came to him: *All the organizations are in this tiny space. Everyone is in this dead end.*

Batons and rifle butts began banging on doors, and cries in a Hebrew accent of 'Open, open up! Now! Open door! Open window! Here, this one! That one! Hurry up!'

'They haven't cut the phone lines, odd,' one of the young men whispered.

'Shhh! Shut up.'

The smell of sweaty bodies, the unbearable weight, the suffocation. One of them yelped, 'Ow! My hand!'

'SHUT IT!'

Silence.

Samar craned her head out the window and yelled, 'They're in Um Hamdallah's house!' She quickly shut it.

The young men heard the fracas, the beating of a door, and finally it being smashed in. They kept quiet.

Um Hamdallah stood tall, blocking the door to her children's bedroom. Trying to shove her to the side, the soldier gruffly ordered, 'Move.'

'I'm not going to.'

'Move!'

'I'm staying right here.'

He knocked her in the chest.

She clung to the door, shrieking, 'Shame on you! Hitting a woman!'

He stretched his lips wide, baring all his teeth. 'You're not woman. You're not even human.' He knocked her a second time and she threw her body on him, latching onto him. He started pummelling her. Her two girls jumped from behind her and attacked him. Two other soldiers came to help. They all were locked together.

Sitt Zakia stood behind the upstairs window and peered downwards. The alley was crawling with soldiers, searchlights and jeeps. Hearing the yells, her heart began to pound like a panicked child. *Your protection, O God. Your protection, O God. Protect us!* From the window she saw Samar snaking her way out from behind the dome of the oven, making her way towards Um Hamdallah's roof, with Um Sadiq in tow. Two soldiers burst forth from the night and started to beat up the two women. One of them grabbed Samar's hair, her head looking like an orange in his Herculean fist. Um Hamdallah ran at him, flinging her entire weight onto his back. The second soldier kicked her but she didn't move, remaining stuck to the first soldier, squeezing his neck until he slackened his grip. Um Mohammed and three other women arrived on the scene, armed with planks of wood. One of the soldiers fell in the gap between the houses. Before he could come to, the hands of the young men shot out to seize him and strangled him. They stretched out his body beneath them and laid on top. One of them chuckled hysterically, 'Look at us, all in this place, sleeping on a dead body. For God's sake!'

'Silence!'

Another one began to whimper. He was still a child, only twelve. Perhaps even younger.

'Shut his mouth! What's happened?'

Choking, he spluttered, 'It's the dead man. He stinks.'

They all snorted with laughter. A hand reached out and gagged the child's mouth. Another whispered, 'Are you crazy? He hasn't had any time.'

'Neither have we,' the retort came.

'SHHH! Keep it down, you lot.'

With a wooden plank in hand, Samar announced, 'They've jumped onto Sitt Zakia's roof! Get them, ladies!'

They rushed towards the midwife's house; she was sitting on the chaise longue, her back against a barrel full of sprouting jasmine, face dazed as she stared at the soldiers leaping in front of her like spirits of fire and destruction. Climbing up the stairs, coming down, flinging open doors, pounding on windowpanes and shattering the glass. Two of them were in the bathroom, two in front of the fridge, their rifles pointed at the fruit bowl and water bottles. Another was whacking the headboard of the bed after having already damaged the other end. A third smashed the perfume bottles.

'What a loss! Why have you done that, my boy?' Sitt Zakia murmured regretfully.

He stood looking at her for a moment. When her eyes met his, he lowered his and rushed towards the stairs leading to the roof to block the women from coming in and attacking. He was clubbed with a wooden plank. He grabbed the weapon from Samar who tumbled down and landed in a heap at Sitt Zakia's feet. She trembled but didn't cry. 'I swear to God, I'll show them.' She stood up, dusted off her behind, then shot forth like a missile.

* * *

'I'm telling you, he stinks!' the boy said.

'Shut up you, wait till they're gone.'

'They *are* gone!'

'No, I think they're at the plumber's house.'

'Still in the quarter?'

'Yes!'

'And the women?'

'Right behind them.'

One of them snorted. 'And here we are on top of a dead man.'

'Shut it, will you? Now's not the time to chat. Keep your mind busy and think.'

Hussam prodded his leg that had fallen asleep and thought of his time in solitary in prison. He had sat there, in that tomb, thinking of everything except his body. 'Free yourself of your body. That's the first lesson,' Samih had advised him. 'Slip it off like you're taking off a shirt.' After having read the message, he ripped it up into little pieces that he stuffed in his mouth and swallowed. They settled, heavy, in his stomach. How easy it is to write words. How easy it is to swallow them. 'Take off your body.' But he wasn't able to, so they did it for him. They beat him until his bones broke. His hands were cuffed behind his back. Electronic handcuffs that automatically tightened at the slightest movement.

This first lesson had been at the monstrous Al-Faria prison. Everything in it was imposing, even the way they cracked bones. No bone was left that hadn't grasped the lesson. At the slightest movement, the handcuffs tightened. In Jenin prison, he didn't make the same mistake. He learnt to hold his breath and think of anything but his body: the library, the lamp trinkets swaying in the breeze, the room by the roof, the hills of Zawata, the gusts of wind and Mount Rubeen. And she, well she was as she always had been, with the most beautiful and beloved name. 'What's your name?' he had asked.

'Sahab.'

Cloud, he thought to himself. 'My God! Sahab! What a wonderful name that commands attention.'

'How so?'

'It reminds me of a proverb we learnt as children at school: Clouds aren't hurt by snapping dogs. How true, how true! Clouds can't be hurt.'

'Exactly,' Samih had agreed. 'No one can hurt a cloud. You, you're a cloud. Remember, this is the second lesson. When you take off your body, you become a cloud, like the wind that someone is trying to get hold of. But no one can ever catch air. Same thing with a cloud.'

Hussam moved his lips without groaning. 'Sahab, Sahab.'

Samar appeared in the window frame and yelled, 'They've gone! But they're still searching the quarter.'

One of the young men jumped out of hiding, opened his fly and pissed. The boy who had been scared opened his mouth and started to vomit. As for Hussam, he sat in a dark corner and let his gaze get lost in space, up towards the stars.

12

After the disappearance of the soldier, the army cordoned off all the openings to the alleyways and started to comb through the neighbourhood. The young men knew all the passageways, the nooks and crannies of every alley, basement and sewer opening. A brutal manhunt began. The young men started a skirmish in the next-door alley. Sitt Zakia's roof filled up with marbles, stones and empty cartridges. Then there was tear gas, fumes from bombs, onion and lemon compresses for protection. People shut their windows and blocked their noses with cologne-soaked handkerchiefs till they grew faint. The young men decided to retreat and leave the quarter. Only the women, children and old men stayed behind.

Hussam, whose thigh was injured, threw himself into Sakina's garden, hiding among the shadows of the poppies and climbing plants. When night descended, he crawled up the stone steps and tapped on the door. When no one answered, he scribbled on a scrap of paper—*Open up Nuzha. – Hussam*—and slipped it under the door. The minutes dragged until she opened it, but in the end she did. Hussam crawled inside to hide himself in Sakina's house.

He stood in front of the bureau, staring at how pale he was. He was coated in dust, his beard scraggy, his eyes jutting out. When he saw Nuzha's reflection in the mirror, he lowered his eyes and commanded, 'Help me.' She remained baffled for a few moments, then rushed towards him, throwing herself on him, almost causing him to lose his balance. But she held him against her young body and supported his weight on her shoulder as they made their way to the sofa, where his aunt had sat just a few days before. In the same terse tone, he said, 'Get me scissors, cotton and iodine.' She leapt up like a teacher's pet to fetch what he needed. She brought it all to him and stood waiting for her next orders.

As he cut the fabric away from the injury, she turned her face away. He glared at her, hostile, as if he were insulting her. 'Scared, are you? You of all people, Nuzha, Sakina's girl, from this scandalous house, this house of naked women, drugs and spies? You're scared? Oh, it hurts so much . . . ' he moaned in pain. She couldn't bear to look and started to back away. 'Where are you going?'

'To make you some tea.'

'No, come here.'

She hastened back.

'Hold the bandage. Press your hand here. Give me the iodine. The cotton. Wrap the gauze. Tie it here. Tighter, tighter! I'm telling you, pull!'

Ah! The procedure was done. He closed his eyes and leant his head against the edge of the couch and dozed off. She stayed sitting at his feet just as she had done before with his aunt. She kept silent, waiting for the slightest sign from him.

13

Wrapping the new bandage around his thigh, she said to him, 'If you hadn't been wounded, I would never have seen you here.'

He didn't engage. He was deep in thought, planning his escape. But how to get away? The soldiers had closed off the entrance of the alley leading to Bab Al-Saha with a wall of metal and cement patrolled by armed men. They had imposed a curfew and, while the quarter was deserted, they had erected this familiar barrier: barrels filled with scraps of metal and cement piled on top of one another until the alley was completely blocked off. At the other end they had set up a checkpoint with an enormous flag draping down, covering the windows of the last house and preventing any light from reaching those who lived inside. No one could come in or go out without being searched and having their ID cards scrutinized.

Ripping up the soiled bandage, Nuzha said, 'I just saw your aunt at the grocer's.'

'You went out?' He scowled. 'When?'

'You were sleeping.'

'You can't go outside. Got it?'

'And what will we eat?'

'I'll take care of it.'

She didn't react but made her way to the kitchen, returning a few minutes later. She sat on the couch, at a distance, embroidering. In a tone that one might use with a friend, she said, 'I was thinking of letting your aunt know that you're at my place and that you're doing okay.'

'And why didn't you?'

'I said good morning to her and she didn't reply.'

'Maybe she didn't hear you.'

'Oh she heard me all right! Probably she's worried about what people will say.'

For the first time, he felt sorry for her, but he pushed the feeling aside and went back to thinking of a way to get out of this prison. He asked her, 'What does the entrance to the alley look like?'

'It's crawling with soldiers. They're frisking everyone, going and coming.'

He fell silent, so she kept silent, too. Then she started up again, as if she were talking to herself. 'Um Hamdallah speaks to me, and Samar too—Um Sadiq's daughter—but your aunt won't even look at me.' She sighed sorrowfully. 'But I know why.' After being quiet for a moment, she asked him, 'Do you want to watch some TV?'

'No.'

'Coffee?'

'No.'

'Tea, then?'

'No.'

'Then what do you want?'

'I want you to shut up.'

She didn't react. He turned to her and saw her face was waxen-white. He felt regretful and grumbled, 'Okay then, get me something to read.'

She turned slowly, then disappeared. He heard her opening doors, drawers, turning things upside down, rummaging through the bureau. First in one room, then the second, then the third. Finally she came to him with a pile of magazines: Al-Maw'id, Al-Shabaka, Al Burda. He smiled, shaking his head.

'That's all I could find!' she flashed.

He shook his head again. 'Fine.'

She turned to put the magazines back where they had come from when he called out to her, 'Come here, give them to me.'

She put the pile on the table in front of him and stepped back. For the first time, he noticed the colour of her dressing gown: a garish yellowish amber.

'Do you stay all day in that thing?' he asked, nearly speechless at how affronted his sensibilities were.

'What do you expect me to wear?'

Hearing no response from him, she receded into her bedroom. When she came out she was wearing a black skirt and a white blouse. She looked as innocent as a schoolgirl. She stood watching him as he paged through the magazines, bored. Raising his head, he stared hard at her.

'What should we . . . what do you want to eat?' she spluttered.

'Soup.'

'Soup? Every day?'

'What's wrong with that?'

'Nothing. Okay, soup it is, then.' She turned away. At lunchtime she came with a tray in her hands: soup with a plate of olives and a hunk of bread on the side. She set it down on the table in front of him and retreated to the kitchen. When he had finished, she brought him a cup of tea and left once more. The same thing happened on the second day.

14

In the evening, they stayed up late watching television. When scenes of the Intifada flashed across the screen during the news bulletin, his curiosity got the better of him. 'What do you think?'

'About what?'

'About what we're watching.'

'You want to hear what I think?'

'Of course.'

'Now, you're saying "of course"?'

He turned to her and saw her face flushed with feeling.

'I asked hundreds of times to see you. I begged your aunt, kissed her hands and feet, I made her swear to God, Mohammed and all that she holds dear, but it was no use. Even before, before I spoke to her, I used to say good morning and she'd respond. But now, when I say it, she pretends that she can't hear me! What's happening to the world? What's happening to people? If this is what the Intifada is, then I don't want it.'

'It's not you who gets to decide,' he said icily.

'Then who? You?'

'Not me either.'

'Or is it those boys who've dropped out of school, roaming the streets showing off their knives and daggers?'

He stared at her, bristling at her insolence.

She tackled him head on. 'What's that dirty look for? Don't like what I said?'

'It's not just that I don't like it. It's just surprising. Surprising how you dare to talk like that, after everything that's happened to you. But after all, you're a . . .' He stopped short.

'Go on, go on. Piece of shit? A whore? A traitor's daughter? A traitor?'

He carried on staring, his mouth agape.

She went on defiantly. 'It couldn't be any worse for me than it is now. You've all gone and stabbed my mother, crushed me, beat me black and blue. You've forgotten that I was in prison just like all of you.'

'And you were released on caution.'

'And Asim Marbout, how was he let out? Now he's throwing his weight around everywhere. It's true what they say, "There are two bitter truths that nobody cares about: a poor man who's dead and a rich man who's crooked."'

He continued to scrutinize her. Such an innocent face coupled with an obscene tongue and filthy acts. Who would have thought that such a face could say such things!

She kept on going, her voice a wave gaining momentum, getting higher and higher. 'Even if you all had a score to settle with my mother, what makes you think you could take it out on me?'

'You're saying you didn't know?'

'And how would I?'

'But you're her daughter.'

'And my brother, who's one of you, is also her son.'

'You lived with her, you *must* have known.'

'From the day I got out of prison, I didn't care about politics and I didn't want to know any more about it. Why back myself into a corner? For someone like Marbout who climbs the ladder and leaves me in the dirt? Go on, ask whoever you want, they'll tell you which one of us grassed up your group.'

'Now's not the time to ask questions and dig up all these stories.'

'So why dig up my story then?'

'Because of your mother.'

Overcome with hysteria, she clamoured, 'Why'd you tar me with the same brush? What about my brother?'

'You're a part of this household.'

'And what about this household? Since the first day of the Intifada, it hasn't welcomed any strangers.'

'And before the Intifada? Every day, someone new.'

'Including your dad!'

He stood up in one swift motion, his hand raised unknowingly, 'Shut the hell up. Don't you talk about my father like that.'

She raised her hand to block his blow. They remained like statues, each eyeing the other. Hussam broke the spell by flopping down onto the sofa gasping, 'Go. Get out of my sight.'

She lowered the hand shielding her and looked at him.

Without looking at her, in a strangled voice, he wheezed, 'Get . . . out . . . of . . . here. GO!'

15

Hussam regained consciousness. *But what has the Intifada done to us? Is it the Intifada or this tension, this homelessness, this floundering? Of course it's a war. Even worse is that people don't think of it as one. But how else would you describe what we're surviving? Since we haven't been able to hurt the other side, we've started hurting ourselves. Raise my hand to a woman? And so what if she had badmouthed my father? Doesn't he deserve it? Of course he does! But not by people like Nuzha. Someone like him shouldn't even be part of such a conversation. He's stingy, yes. Cruel, yes. Hot-tempered, selfish, opportunistic, takes advantage of others—but he's not a traitor. People like Nuzha should understand that. Spying is nothing like business, giving up young men is not like handing over some goods, and selling land is not the same as selling the heads of wanted men. As for that land, in any case, no one had ever proved that he'd sold it, and who would prove it now?*

He clearly remembered the day his father sold some of the land next to Zawata to complete the house. His uncle, a government advisor, had come from Kuwait and quarrelled with his father. He was so young then, too young to know exactly the words flung back and forth. All he remembered was that his uncle left their house and went to stay with Sitt

Zakia in Bab Al-Saha. He saw everyone in the house going and coming, entering the guest rooms, shutting the doors behind them, shouting at the top of their lungs, 'The land! The land!'

None of the whispers, slander or condemnations was ever proven. As such, it was futile to bring it back up now. But people like Nuzha liked to pick at such scabs, saying, 'No one is better than anyone else. We sell for shekels, and you for dinars. We sell for petty cash, and you sell for thousands.'

He felt strangled, thirsty, but he didn't go to the kitchen. As if he'd drink some of Nuzha's water or raid her fridge! The sounds of their fight still echoed in his head, buzzing like a swarm of mosquitoes. His hand raised above her in the air was like a flame rising, now burning, the flames lapping at his heart. His head caught fire, his throat, then his entire body. He wanted nothing more than a sip of water. He remembered his time in prison and the suffocating heat. He remembered solitary, the shadowy figures and the moans of his fellow inmates. 'Take off your body. Remove it like a piece of clothing,' Samih had said. 'Only your body is in prison but your spirit can't be caught. It's like trying to catch the wind.'

He came to once more. *I'm a prisoner here. Sakina's house is my prison and Nuzha is the guard. Uniforms surround the quarter and here I am caught between the checkpoint and the reinforced-concrete-cum-metal barrier.*

He drew close to the carved wooden window frame, pulled back the curtain and looked out. Nothing but night, pitch-black night, and the walls of the alleyways. At the height of his thirst and burning up he murmured, 'Sahab! Sahab!'

16

Days went by without her speaking to him, let alone looking at him. She would prepare his food at the same time every day, leave it in the same place, then quickly make herself scarce. He would hear her moving about in the bigger rooms, and the spacious living room. The sounds seemed faraway, muffled, no ringing or echoes. The windows were still shut, as were the curtains, and if it hadn't been for the vents higher up, they would have suffocated though it wasn't even hot— in fact, it was the end of winter, the drizzle announcing its departure. The leaves of the lemon tree rustled ominously.

One day he heard the branches moving even more force-fully, the rustling incessant. Then a light tapping on the door leading to the back garden. Nuzha was standing in front of the bureau, her image reflected in the enormous mother of pearl mirror. From where he was, he saw her face blanche and her eyes freeze. She didn't look at him but stayed where she was, anticipating.

The tapping became knocks. Then a thin voice called out and whispered, 'Nuzha, open up! It's me, Samar.'

She looked at him as he put up his hand, signalling for her to wait. He got up from where he was, went into the bedroom and left the door open a crack. Samar entered and he saw her through the crack, shaking out her long, wet hair. Samar turned to Nuzha playfully and said, 'What, Nuzha? You didn't hear me? Well, first off, good morning. How could you not have heard me when I was out there for a whole hour?'

Nuzha said nothing but he saw her distance herself from Samar, making her way to the kitchen. She came back with a towel and a cloth for the floor. She threw the cloth on the floor and said briskly, 'This is for your feet, and this one is for your hair.'

'And if I use them the other way round?' Samar giggled.

It seemed Nuzha wasn't in the mood for jokes. 'Fine,' she responded gravely.

Still by the door, Samar wiped her feet and dried her hair while Nuzha explained why it took so long for her to open to door: the door to the back garden was a long way from the sitting room, and it was only used in exceptional circumstances.

'And I'm an exception,' Samar interrupted her. She quickly realized her faux pas, alluding so clearly to Nuzha's isolation, her neighbours never stopping by. She hastily added, 'I mean, *my project and me* are an exception. Whenever I visit any woman, they always spend an hour asking me what, why and how. Look, the whole thing is that I'm investigating the effects of the Intifada on women's living conditions. Such as, have their responsibilities increased? Has their work changed? I mean . . . has it effected their economic position? Do they earn less than before? And if so, how do they manage?'

Nuzha didn't appear to be interested in the least. 'What's this got to do with me?'

Samar froze for just a moment but then bubbled with enthusiasm. 'I'll just explain, but won't you first invite me in? Invite me in first.'

Nuzha coldly extended her hand out in front of her. 'If you want to come in, come on in.'

Samar quickly glanced over the sitting room, taking everything in. Her eyes settled on the dining table next to the bureau and the door to the back garden. 'Here, this is fine. Before we start, it would be nice to have a coffee. Do you have any coffee?'

'Arabic or Nescafe?'

'You have Nescafe? I think that would go better with this chilly weather, what do you think?'

'Sure,' Nuzha replied curtly.

They disappeared into the kitchen and each came back out with a steaming cup. Hussam wished he were as lucky as one of them, so he could have a drink too and take part in their sit-down, but he stayed where he was, eavesdropping and watching.

Samar went back to explaining the importance of her project—understanding all dimensions of how the Intifada had affected women and the role that women played and so on. But Nuzha still didn't show any interest. Samar persisted in explaining all angles of what she was doing until Nuzha rudely interrupted her. 'Okay, okay, I've got it. But you've got to get it through your head that I'm fed up with the Intifada, women, and with people in general! Don't ask me why, as if you don't already know. You know everything and I know that you know, everyone in the quarter knows. After what's happened to me, I couldn't care less about anyone else or what happens to them. I don't give a shit!'

Samar lowered her head, stunned. Silence ensued.

Nuzha suddenly changed tack. 'Or shall I speak to you? You've made the effort to come here, you're kind, you have a good heart, and you're one of the few people who do actually respond to my "Good morning". I'll work with you then, play your game and give you what you want.'

Samar smiled indulgently. 'Play my game?'

Nuzha shook her hand as if shooing away a fly. 'Don't take it to heart, honey, I say anything and everything.'

'So, you'll answer my questions, then?'

'Every one. Ask me whatever you want. How many clients I have, their names, their addresses, how many children they have, their wives, their bank balances. I'll tell you everything, just ask.'

Samar stared at her, a glint of excitement and interest dancing in her eyes. 'You're certain?' she exclaimed.

'Yes! Just ask the question.'

Samar quickly shuffled through her papers, her breath heavy with anticipation. From where he was, Hussam started breathing just as heavily, burning with curiosity.

'Okay, so first off, I'll start with the usual questions about your age, social status, economic situation, childhood, any problems you've faced. Then afterwards we'll talk about the Intifada.'

'Ask me *whatever* you want,' Nuzha said flatly, her eyes fixed on the wall in front of her.

Samar assumed the stance of a researcher. 'Your name?'

'It's Nuzha, but you already know that.'

'Nuzha what? Or let's forget about your last name.'

'No, write it, write whatever you want.'

'Forget it, let's move on. Age?'

'Twenty-seven.'

'A year older than me.'

Nuzha said nothing.

'How many people in your family?'

'Seven.'

'That's how many brothers and sisters you have?'

'No. My mum's dead and my dad too. But you know that. There are three of us girls and two boys.'

'And are all your brothers and sisters are still alive?'

'Exactly. My two sisters are married, one in Zarqa and the other in Saudi Arabia. God's taken care of them, thankfully.

My elder brother ran away to America and the younger is in the mountains. And me, as you see now, I'm just here.'

'You live alone?'

'Completely. No one cares about me and I don't care about them.'

'And your economic situation?'

'Aha! Now we've really started.'

'If you don't want to answer you don't have to.'

'And why wouldn't I? I'll tell you a story and a half. Look here, sweetheart, before the Intifada we used to be able to put away some *qirsh* for a rainy day. But now with the fall of the dinar, prices going up and jobs being cut left and right, things have become tough. Not a lot tougher, but still, I mean I'm better off then a lot of others. Don't forget that I live alone— the house belongs to us, so I'm only spending money on food. But of course, things aren't how they were before: I had a car, a red BMW to die for, and I used to drive about in it wherever I wanted, till they burnt it, that is, but you already know this! Then they stabbed my mum, and there you go.' She stayed quiet, waiting for more questions while Samar looked at her, trying to take everything in. 'So! Other questions?'

Samar started and looked at her papers. 'Your civil status?'

'My what?'

'Married, single or other?'

'Other.'

'Meaning . . . ?'

'Divorced.'

'You got married and then divorced?'

'Didn't you know that?'

'No I didn't. How would I?'

Nuzha looked at her slyly, a malicious smile playing on her lips, as if to say It's better for you if you don't ask who.

'I swear that I didn't know, I mean, how would I?'

'Okay, okay, I believe you. But I can't get my head around how a woman like you from Nablus, from Bab Al-Saha on top of that, doesn't know everything about everybody, and especially about the people living in this house.'

'Honestly, I didn't know.'

'Fine, I believe you.'

'How old were you when you got married?'

'Fifteen.'

'FIF-TEEN?'

'What? Does that surprise you? Half of the girls from here get married at that age, some even younger.'

'How did you get married?'

'Like everyone else. They made me wear a tulle veil, showed me off on stage, sang and danced for me.'

'No, no. When I said "how", I meant, was it a love marriage or arranged traditionally?'

'It was all completely legal, according to God's law, the Prophet's tradition, registered, with a sheikh. I'm telling you, just like everyone else.'

'No, I want to know, did your husband come to ask for your hand from your family, according to our custom, or did he love you and you loved him?'

'Love me, you say? He wouldn't know the meaning of the word. How would he know how to love and be loved? Damn him!'

'Hold on, slow down. You're saying that you never loved him?'

'Oh darling, what are these questions? He was forty-five, a mule really, marrying a fifteen-year-old girl. And you're asking me about love?'

'It's possible.'

'What do you mean by "It's possible"?'

'As in, just because he's old and like a mule doesn't mean that he doesn't know how to love and want to be loved. The Prophet was fifty-six when he married his wife Aicha who was only nine.'

'Good God, Samar! This is the first time I've heard this. Really?'

'Like I said, he was fifty-six and she was nine. But the way he loved her, he didn't love any of his other wives like that.'

'He understood her.'

'And your husband didn't?'

'He was an animal—an animal! All he was missing was a tail and I was just a small chick, still in her shell. May God forgive my mother! What can I say?'

'She's the one who married you off?'

'After my dad died, we fell on hard times and she married us all off to whoever came along: first come, first served.'

'Because of how poor you all were.'

'Not just that, she was just plain stupid, God help us. She never learnt a thing from what happened to her. She threw each of us into a hole deeper than the next. My sister Sabiha was married off to someone who already had a wife. My other sister Amina to a beast who makes her worship a golden calf, and me, to an old idiot. Both of my sisters have a load of kids hanging around their necks, weighing them down. Strangling them, really.'

'How about you?'

'I had a boy but I dumped him on his father when he was still in nappies, and I escaped.'

'Where to?'

'I ran off with this barber, who turned out to be just as much of an animal and dumped me two months later.'

'Here, in Nablus?'

'No, in Amman. I was married in Amman and when the barber buggered off, I found myself trapped, so I came back here.'

'Why did you run off with him?'

'Back then, I thought I was in love. A good-looking, smarmy bastard with a Lebanese accent. He always wore this bracelet. I was still so young and eager, wanting to love and be loved. I loved him, or I thought I did. Of course my husband was a stupid fool, so I fell hard with no one to catch me. I dumped my son and my husband and took just a few valuables with me and made a run for it.'

'Didn't you consider the risks?'

'Consider? There was no consideration or calculation. I'm like that. I'm not afraid and I don't think too hard about things. I've been like this my whole life—whatever I think of, I do. I've been like this ever since I was at school. When we used to go out on marches, I used to hop over the walls of the boys' schools at Salihiyya, Jahiz, Amiryya and open the gates. They used to call me "Wild Girl", because once ... oh I'll tell you this story that will really make you laugh! This one time on Earth Day, I hopped over the wall to one of the boys' schools and stood in the middle of the field throwing rocks. The principal came out, waddling like a duck. When he saw me there, he slapped his bald head, shook his cane and shouted, "Hey you, wild girl! Which jungle have you come from? Just wait till I catch you. If you don't have a father to discipline you, I'll do it myself." I looked at his bald head shining in the sun like a mirror, his huge belly and his gorilla face, and I said to myself, "Who does he think he is? If he wasn't so bald, I might listen to him. If his belly wasn't so big, then he could really throw his weight around. But he's such a gorilla, everyone hates him. Seriously, who does he think he is? I'll have to show him at thing or two." I looked ahead and saw the boys by the windows, crowded behind the glass like mice. Behind me I saw the gatekeeper holding the hose and watering the garden. I ran up to him, snatched the hose out of his hands and aimed it at the bald principal, shouting:

'Shut your mouth you dirty swine
It's you who lost us Palestine!

'The boys started laughing. They opened the windows and I heard them shout back:

'Shut your mouth you dirty swine
It's you who lost us Palestine!

'I turned the hose on the boys and all hell broke loose. They were jumping on the tables and chairs. The principal was running after me and I was jumping about from one place to another, spraying him the whole time. The boys were all pushing each other and running out of the school. Then someone turned off the water supply. I was afraid the principal would catch me so I ran away from the gatekeeper, dragging the hose behind me. The gatekeeper was chasing me, shouting, "Wild Girl! Give it here, give it here!"'

Samar started laughing, wiping her eyes, repeating, 'Unbelievable!'

Without the slightest smile, Nuzha went on, 'And from that day, whenever any of the boys saw me in the street, they used to shout "Wild Girl! Give it here, give it here!"'

From behind the door, Hussam shook his head sadly. *So you were Wild Girl!* He remembered the scene so crisply as if it were in front of him now. There he stood jostling with the other boys behind the windows to get a better look, then screaming till he went hoarse. So then, the young girl in the blue jumper with the blond mop of hair had been Nuzha. How had he forgotten her?

Samar prodded her to go on. 'What happened next?'

'Well after that, the principal complained to my mum and I got a hiding. But really, what was the point. It wasn't the first time someone complained about me and it wouldn't be the last. Because of that, I couldn't believe it when she married me off. God rest her soul—whatever she might have done to me'.

'So you got along with her, then?'

'Got along? What do you want me to tell you exactly? Ask me if I loved her, if I listened to what she said, if I respected her. If you ask me then I'll tell you.'

'Did you love her?'

'Um . . . yes I did. Why should I deny it? Even now, I still miss her. Whatever people say about her, I don't believe it. My mum, a traitor? A spy? Impossible. The day I was arrested, no one stood by me, they all disappeared, including that shit Asim. But she didn't. She stood by me right to the end. She knew everything and if she had wanted to talk, she would have. But she didn't.'

Hussam wished he could yell from his hiding place, *But she did! She did talk!*

Deeply moved, Nuzha continued, 'If they had had a real trial, they would have known. But there wasn't one. So what can we say about it now?'

Hussam shook his head while still listening in silence. *But we did try her and she confessed.*

'If she had wanted to talk, she would have, but she didn't say anything and neither did I. Asim Marbout is the one who squealed and gave us all up one after the other.'

'Then you got two years and were released on bail.'

'You see! I said you knew.'

'How could I not have known? Everyone was talking about it. But let's not jump ahead. Tell me about your childhood.'

'What about it?'

'Was it happy or not?'

'I'd be lying if I told you it was happy. But I'd also be lying if I told you that it wasn't. It's just that my older brother always used to beat me up.'

'The one in America?'

'Yes, him.'

'And why would he hit you?'

'He used to say that I was rude, badly brought up.'

'Why'd he say that?'

'Because he was jealous! I was pretty and graceful, like the moon. Everyone who saw me wanted me.'

'You're still pretty.'

'Oh you haven't seen anything. Back then, Najla Fathi, Mervet Amine and Souhair Ramzi had nothing on me! I used to dance and dance—it's crazy that I used to dance as well as I did. I wanted to be an actress but I didn't know where to start. What did other people have that I didn't? I used to leave my mum when she was sewing and steal one of her sparkly dresses. I used to put it on, tighten the sash and stand in front of the mirror, moving this way and that. I used to put the radio on full blast. My mum used to come over, sit down and be happy for a moment while she was watching me, forgetting the world and everything in it. One time, my brother suddenly came out of nowhere and started punching me. He was raving like a madman, saying I was loose, depraved, shameless, other things like that. When Mum tried to calm him down, he turned on her and said, "This is all your fault. You taught her to like music and dance. You taught her that it was okay to behave like this." My God! In the end, he upped and left for America and we were free from his evil clutches. He used to put us down and pretend that he was some big sheikh or something. He could do no wrong. But when he was in his own world in Israel, he did whatever the hell he liked. He used to bring these girls back with him who'd sit in the back garden smoking hashish till the morning. So *he'd* given in to the seven deadly sins but, as far as we were concerned, he played the religious bigot. Such a hypocrite!'

'And your other brother?'

'You mean Ahmed? He was a baby, barely out of nappies. When Dad died, Ahmed was still a baby and I was ten. May he rest in peace. The day he died, our whole world turned upside down and everything changed. My mother changed, my brother changed, I changed, even our house did. For two or three years we were living off handouts. Mum hadn't gone to school, wasn't streetwise, wasn't good at sewing or embroidering and couldn't do any real work other than wiping things down, tidying up and cleaning windows. Her whole life she'd never had a real job, and because of that she never got the hang of sewing, embroidery or anything else. She didn't want to clean other people's homes. So we ended up living through dark days, blacker than tarmac. She pulled my brother out of school and put him to work plastering and painting houses. Then he started going to Israel to work, spending what he wanted, bringing us back whatever was left, and started smoking hashish. Then he ran off to America, left us on all on our own in this hellhole.'

'And when you turned fifteen, she married you off?'

'No, hold on. Before I got married, I worked.'

'Doing what?'

'Well first, I made a living breaking almonds, then I was in the bakery with your brothers and after that at Zizi Studio.'

'You worked at Zizi?'

'Yes, I did.'

Samar fell quiet. All that she had heard about that place sprang to mind: girls posing naked, depraved morals, prostitution, spies. She didn't move or make any comment.

It was Nuzha who broke the silence. 'Of course, you want to know what I was doing there.'

Samar thought for a bit. 'No, no, not now. We can talk about Zizi later.'

'Later, when?'

'Later.'

Nuzha's mood grew dark and she stubbornly insisted, 'No, I want to talk to you about Zizi Studio *now*.'

Samar smiled. The two women sized each other up. Defiantly, Nuzha pushed, 'What, you don't like me?'

'If I didn't like you, I wouldn't be here in the first place.'

Nuzha stared closely at Samar once more. Her delicate features, her smooth skin, her clear eyes. She shook her head bitterly. 'You're all the same. You, Hussam, Asim Marbout, all of you. From outside you're smooth and slick but inside you're rotten. All of you, you're all the same.'

Trying to change the subject, Samar said, 'So you said you worked at the bakery with my brothers.'

Nuzha bit her lip, then answered tersely, 'Uh-huh.'

'And what did you do there?'

'I stuffed the pastries with dates. I would pit them, knead them with cinnamon and prepare them as a filling.'

'And why did you leave?'

Nuzha did not reply right away, as if she were weighing her words.

'And why did you leave?' Samar pressed.

Nuzha made a dismissive motion with her hands, then smiled wickedly, 'You can't ask this question.'

Burning with curiosity, Samar prodded, 'Tell me why. I won't tell anyone.'

Nuzha scrutinized her anew. Suspicion bubbled at the surface as lava would at the mouth of a volcano. She felt an intense resentment that she couldn't place or explain why she felt it.

'No, I don't want to say.' She looked in the direction of the room where Hussam was sleeping and twisted her mouth.

'Fine, if that's what you want,' Samar gave in, dejected. She shuffled her papers trying to establish some sense of calm. 'Whatever suits you. If you don't feel comfortable answering a question, you don't have to.'

Nuzha examined her, smiling sarcastically. 'Hah, that's clever.' She took in the pile of papers in front of the young woman, the pen in hand, and grew angry. 'Research? What research? Let's see what you could possibly want from me. Of course you want to know why I've ended up like this. And why Mum went the way she did. And why our house ended up the way it is. Research? The pleasure is all mine, Madame Researcher!' Then she took aim and fired off mean-spiritedly. 'Sure, I was young at the time, but I got a grip of things mid-flight, understood how the world works. I said to myself, "If I've got to do *that*, why do it with men at the bakery when I can do it with class?"'

Samar's eyes opened wide in surprise. 'That? What's *that*?'

Nuzha smiled. She bit the tip of her tongue and hissed, 'That. Don't you know?'

Samar didn't respond. She kept staring.

Hussam started to twitch behind the door. He felt it wasn't a fair fight between the two girls. Or more precisely, between that naive girl and that evil woman. Maybe she really was just pure evil, or maybe she was a product of her circumstances and what had happened to her. Maybe her reasons were much more complicated than people had thought, but the result in any case was the same. In such a situation, when your back is up against the wall, you don't have time to be a saint, to think of Mary Magdalene or offer your left cheek.

Here you are, Hussam, in a right pickle. You're being chased but the way out is blocked. What if they slap you with the label of victim? You're the victim and the executioner. Sacrifice the victim for the sake of tomorrow. He had to focus now on saving Samar—but how?

He heard her voice, a little bit hoarse as if she had suddenly been struck with a cold. 'I get you, really, I do. Life hasn't been a bed of roses for you. But try to make an effort here to get where I'm coming from, too.'

Hussam wished he could scream bloody murder: *You can't take her on, Samar, you can't take her on!* But he remained silent, tongue-tied, hidden, his hands bound.

'I believe in people, Nuzha,' Samar gushed sincerely. 'I believe in you, in this quarter, in this entire country. Don't you believe in anything, Nuzha?'

Nuzha contemplated her for some time but didn't respond. She thought, disgusted, *What's this shit I have to put up with? This is the last thing I need right now.*

Samar went on, her voice climbing. 'You don't have to believe in anything, Nuzha, but I do. I have faith. Don't think that I believe because I'm coming from a place of power, no. I'm not from Al-Shwetireh or Bleibus. I'm from here, Bab Al-Saha, and the cobblestones of these alleys have made my heels rough and ragged. When your mother used to stop you all from playing with us in the quarter, my brothers and I, we waded through the mud up to our knees. Yes, I'm the daughter of a baker, my brothers are bakers, true, and we're surviving on God's blessings and that of the bakery. Our family is known as "the bakers", meaning you're talking to the baker's daughter and the baker's daughter is at your service.'

'Why on earth are you telling me all this? What did I say?'

Samar's face flushed red but she tried to remain poised. Stiffly, she said, 'You hinted at some things and I understood what you were trying to say.'

'What did you understand?'

'I understood what I understood. Let's drop it.'

'Aha! I see that you're annoyed. I didn't want to ruffle your feathers and that's why I didn't say why I left your brothers.'

'Nuzha! Just forget it.'

'I just want you to understand me.'

There was a heavy silence. Hussam fell flat on the ground, his joints finally loosening up. *God be praised*, he thought. Then he smiled, shaking his head, God be praised! He went back to peeping through the crack to see her features, and he saw Samar's profile, tapered like the blade of a knife. He was taken aback and thought worriedly, Is *that really Samar's face?* He went back to look again and check. This time he didn't see anything. Her silky hair was completely covering one side of her face. He saw her stretch her fingers, comb them through her locks to bring them back and tilt her head to one side. Now he saw her whole face—not just one but both halves. Dumfounded, he stared. When she spoke, he saw her extend her hand and touch that of her peer's, saying kindly, 'How about we pause here?' When she didn't get a response, she suggested, 'How about some more coffee?'

'Why not?' Nuzha frostily acquiesced, her response laced with a grimace.

17

The two women drank coffee in the kitchen—Arabic this time. Hussam caught a whiff of its rich aroma from afar and fell deep into depression once more. Before his fight with Nuzha, he had dared to ask her for a cup of tea; now, for many long days, he hadn't had a drop of tea or coffee.

He stayed where he was on the ground, behind the door, waiting for more. Finally they came back, smiling like old chums. Heaving a sigh of relief, he hoped that the conversation would turn to other things. Even if it wasn't anything worthwhile, at least something to distract him and make him forget this damned wound. Listening to their chatter was without a doubt better than bearing the pain in the melancholy silence of the house. This wretched house, this ghastly house, this house and its wicked memories, its loathsome past. This horrible pain and this blasted wound!

Nuzha started to chuckle. 'Go on, ask me. I swear this time I'll do exactly what you want and more. I mean you're my guest, after all. Even more than that, you're the only person who dared to enter my house of your own free will.'

'People have been forced to come in against their will?' Samar giggled.

Nuzha's eyes darted in the direction of Hussam's room as she deviously replied, 'But of course!'

A furious Hussam's mouth stretched into a tight-lipped smile. *Hah! The whore, child of a whore!* But what could he do in his state, anyway?

Samar began seriously, 'Before we move onto the Intifada, let's talk about something you like.'

'Like what?'

'Anything.'

'Like a person? Or a thing?'

'Whatever you want.'

Nuzha thought for a bit then said slowly, 'I love two things in life, nothing else.'

'What are they?'

'The first is fashion. The second, my little brother Ahmed. Or actually the other way round, my God, yes: first Ahmed, then fashion.

'And your son?'

'He's been dead for a while now. Two weeks after I ran away. I didn't feel anything for him. God curse me. I swear, I don't know why I didn't feel anything. Maybe because I was so young, maybe because I was so head over heels with that barber and not aware of anything else around me. I don't know! Sometimes when I see just how awful and unfeeling I am, I say to myself: Why am I like this? Why doesn't any one love me? And why can't I love them? Fine, so no one loves me, but why can't I care about people? I couldn't even mourn my own son!'

'But you felt your mother's death,' Samar countered tenderly.

'I didn't just feel it, it burnt me alive.'

'And you love Palestine.'

'Hyuk, hyuk, hyuk!' Nuzha snorted. 'Palestine? Don't make me laugh!'

'Why? Didn't you say that you went out and protested?'

'Sweetheart! That was child's play. I didn't know what I was doing. It was all about running, throwing rocks, jumping over walls, dragging garden hoses. Nothing but child's play.'

'And later on, you were arrested.'

'Ah, yes. I was arrested, had to stomach a lot, but I didn't grass anyone up.'

'And that's not love?'

'Yes and no. Love for Marbout but not for Palestine. When I started playing around with politics, I didn't play the game to free the country. Shit, and more shit. I don't care about any of it! But when I loved him, the bastard, I lost my way. I got confused, unsure of how to please him any more. He told me, go to Natania, I went. Go to Tel Aviv, I went. Seduce the officers, I did it. Buy weapons, I bought them. Hide the weapons, I stashed them. If he had told me to go to India, or even Mars, I would have done it. I loved him, I'm telling you, I really did.'

'As much as the barber?'

'More, more. More than my life itself, than Mum, more than daylight.'

'More than Ahmed?'

'Ahmed is different. He's my brother, the light of my eyes. I brought him up, like my own son. He's the last of us and the best of us. Ahmed is my soul . . . ' Her voice broke. 'Ahmed . . . oh Ahmed.' She burst out sobbing.

Tears sprang from Samar's eyes, too. Gradually they pulled themselves together and dabbed their cheeks.

Nuzha said, her voice still swinging high and low, 'You see how life is? You see where Ahmed is and where we are? Who would believe it? Who would have thought? My big brother is lost in America, and Ahmed in the mountains with the shepherds, me here in this house, and Mum in her grave. Worse than a grave, a damn hole is what it is. And this house, you see what's gone on in it, and here I am buried alive.'

And I'm a prisoner of this grave, Hussam thought as he shook his head sorrowfully.

Nuzha scanned the living room, her eyes resting on the velvet curtains, the furniture inlaid with mother of pearl and the crystal ornaments. 'If only you could have seen what this house was like! It was out of this world, a heaven really. Paradise. At night, it was the stuff of dreams. Don't you dare believe those people that say that there were only Jews here, no man from here can say that he didn't live it up in here.'

Samar paused to think. 'Because of the Jews?'

'No! It wasn't just the Jews letting loose. The men from here did stupid things and said it was because of the Jews. When they want to hide their bullshit, they say it's the Jews. When they're embarrassed of what they've done, they blame the Jews. Not everyone who came here was a Jew.'

Samar looked at her, stupefied. What could she say or do? Have a debate with Nuzha? She was completely at a loss for words. Nuzha too, it seemed. Hussam craned his ear closer to the door, until his head almost popped out, but he didn't hear a thing. He saw Nuzha staring down his door. She suddenly leapt up out of her chair, pushed it to one side and ran towards her scarlet bedroom, coming back with a mother-of-pearl jewellery box. She placed it on the table under the chandelier. When she lifted the lid, the sparkle of diamonds and other precious stones spilt forth. She plucked out a weighty bracelet.

'See this? From Haj Iskander. And this? From Dr Uthman. And this one? From Sheikh Ishaq. And how about this? From Majid the lawyer. This, this and this, all from Marbout. She looked towards the door behind which Hussam was and let out a dramatic sigh, 'Ah . . . look at this beauty, this chandelier above our heads and the crystal—guess who gave them?' Samar tilted her head upwards and eyed the huge chandelier. 'I haven't got a clue,' she whispered.

'From Mr Wajih Abdel Qadir himself.'

'Sitt Zakia's brother?'

'That's the one.'

Hussam crumpled to his knees, causing his wound to tear open and blood to seep out. *You bitch! You bitch!*

'I can't believe it!' Samar exclaimed incredulously. 'He's so stingy and everyone knows it.'

Gloating, Nuzha corrected her, 'When it comes to his wife maybe, his children yes, his country sure, but not when it comes to me. Here, in this house, he'd forget himself. Hah, hah, hah!'

'You little bitch, even death is too good for you,' Hussam breathed through clenched teeth. He decided then and there that he would leave her house even if he had to crawl on his belly. But his wound kept oozing, more and more. How could he escape?

18

They both heard a loud sound that jolted the crystal chandelier, causing it to tinkle. 'Good God!' Nuzha gasped.

Samar stared wide-eyed, her face draining of colour. 'They've stormed the quarter!' Another shock made the shutters vibrate as if they were being bombed. Nuzha screwed up her eyes and listened ever so carefully. 'No, it's not an attack.' Then there was a third rumble and the sound of rocks crashing down.

Samar let out a cry. 'The barrier!' She sprung to her feet, clenching her fists against her chest. 'They've knocked the barrier down, they've knocked it down!' She pushed her chair behind her and stood in the middle of the sitting room, looking round in all directions. Overcome by curiosity, Nuzha stood up as well. She rushed towards the kitchen, calling out behind her, 'Come see!' From the kitchen window, they saw the collapsed barrier, only its base still in place. The barrels full of cement were strewn on the ground like lifeless corpses while children circled round them, hopping, skipping and chanting, 'They've knocked it down, they've knocked it down!'

A voice from Sitt Zakia's rooftop rang out, 'Bring in the barrels, bring them in!' The alley reverberated with the children's squeals and women's ululations.

While adjusting the shutters, Samar saw a masked man signalling to the children from the rooftop. 'That's Hussam, it's got to be him,' she whispered.

Nuzha smiled deviously. 'Really, now?'

'Yes, it's him. Definitely Hussam.'

Nuzha let out a yelp of laughter, her shoulders shaking and squirming. 'Whatever you say, it must be Hussam.' She let out a low purr of satisfaction.

Rocks started pelting down like raindrops and shots resounded in nearby alleys.

Nuzha pushed in a hidden door behind the fridge. It opened, complaining, creaking loudly. A dark room came into view from behind the door, the smell of stored onions, garlic and other dried goods wafting out. She stepped into the room, orienting herself towards the wall facing Bab Al-Saha. She opened the shutters of the skylight as small as a hatch, allowing a slender beam of pale light to filter through. The sky was still overcast despite the rain having stopped, the sun masked by the clouds. Samar came in behind Nuzha and stood in the middle of the dome-shaped room with stone arches and a low ceiling. She saw shelves bursting with sacks, cans of oil and long braids of garlic. She felt the walls, wondering aloud, 'Which room is *this*?'

Still peering out from the skylight, an intrigued Nuzha informed her, 'It was a cowshed that we divided into two and made into a storeroom. The second part is hidden underground.' Suddenly she let out a cry. 'Oh my God! They've killed a Jew! Killed him they have, killed him!'

Samar darted to the skylight. Nuzha made space for her, still shrieking, worked up. 'Look, look, they've spread him out on the roof like a bag of olives. The masked man on Sitt Zakia's roof is the one who did it. My God, what a horrible scene!' She had barely finished her sentence when explosions and machine guns went off in tandem.

Rocks started flying every which way in the sky over Bab Al-Saha, ricocheting off the age-old town clock, the top of the citadel and domes of the mosque. A group of masked men raced out, running in every direction throughout the square, disappearing into the side alleys, with soldiers in hot pursuit. The air was soon saturated with gas, so Nuzha shut the opening in the storeroom. She picked up an onion, crushed it under her heel and offered half of it to Samar. She swept out of the room, ordering Samar, 'Come inside!'

Within moments they were in the sitting room, each one splayed out on the sofa with half an onion in one hand and a handful of tissue paper in the other. The clash went on for more than an hour. They didn't dare look out the window or open the shutters because even the air inside the house was heavy with gas and smoke. Their throats were on fire. The loudspeakers announced that curfew was in place and a few minutes later the soldiers started their inspection rounds: breaking in windows, bashing down doors and beating up those who lived there.

Samar looked round the huge room once more: the artfully carved wooden pieces of furniture, the velvet curtains ... and remembered that she was in Sakina's home. With the curfew in place, she would be a hostage here for several days, at the very least. She murmured, growing panicked as she realized this. 'What a trap! I'm done for!'

Nuzha looked at her hard, her eyebrows dancing in delight, her satisfaction evident. 'Welcome Samar!' she chanted in a singsong voice. 'And then there were three!'

19

He opened his eyes and saw the curtains dancing, dark silhouettes, khaki uniforms, the walls of his cell, then flames.
He heard the racket of machines, his comrades moaning. His
head felt heavier than a rock. And the fire kept blazing, not
dying down for a moment.

Samar laid a new compress across his forehead. 'He's
going to die, he must see a doctor,' she said anxiously.

Nuzha looked at him for some time, her back to the cup-
board mirror. Irritated, she said, 'What a crock of shit! He
couldn't find anywhere else to die but here?' She turned, her
eyes meeting Samar's in the mirror. 'It's all my fault the, poor
bugger,' she mumbled. 'All my fault.' She felt her face and
came across a small wrinkle in the delicate skin by her right
eye. 'Every day a new one,' she sighed sorrowfully. This time
she didn't think of getting work done in the Hadasa hospital
—as her mum used to say—but instead thought of her life
rolling on, never stopping, and her future limited to strikes,
mourning and curfews. No work, no hobbies, no real home
or children, no prince charming to save her from drowning.

Hussam's moaning startled her, bringing her back to
reality. She grew sad remembering his hand raised to strike
her face and how she didn't feel resentment but disappoint-
ment. She had hoped, she had wished for so much. Hadn't
she heard about him? About how clever he was? About his
big heart? About his love for the carpenter's daughter? The

carpenter's daughter was a princess, smiling at her subjects as she paraded past. A princess she was, so this man had to be a prince. But he wasn't! He had his nose in the air like all men, a big look-at-me!

'You have any vinegar?' Samar inquired.

'No, but I've got arrack.'

'Okay, give me that, maybe it'll be useful.'

'It'll work, it'll work. There's nothing better!'

He opened his eyes and groaned, 'Water, water . . . just a drop.'

Samar leant into him, feeling his blistering hot breaths on her face. 'I'm Samar, the baker's daughter,' she said tenderly.

'Water, water, just a drop.'

Nuzha came back with the arrack, water and a bucket of ice. Samar wet the compress with arrack and ice and then gave him some water to swallow. 'Try to sleep,' she said tenderly.

Nuzha began to have pity on him. 'Haram! It's so unfair! He's so young!'

Samar shook her head, lost in thought. He's got to see a doctor. We need an ambulance, right now. 'Nuzha, he needs a doctor.'

'Where are we going to find a doctor with this curfew?'

'How about calling an ambulance?'

'If we call one, they'll find out where he's been hiding. He's so young!' Nuzha examined his flushed face and felt sorry. 'You know what? My conscience is killing me, I left him the whole day without a bite,' she confessed.

'The whole day!'

'Yes, the whole damn day.'

'Shame on you! You're heartless.'

'It wasn't on purpose. I was busy with you and the curfew.'

'No, it was on purpose. You hate him. Come on, admit it!'

'Okay, yes, I hated him, but not all the time. I hated him when he raised his hand to hit me . . . yes, I hated him then.'

'And you still hate him.'

'Not all the time, I swear on my mum. Sometimes I hated him and other times I would say he's one of the good ones. I have heard so much about him and how clever he is. Everyone says he's sound.'

'Yes, they do.'

'So then why haven't you fallen for him already?'

Samar turned to her, taken by surprise.

Nuzha pressed on, 'Yes, why don't you love him? Why should it be Sahab? *Wallah*, you're nicer to look at.'

Samar shook her head compassionately, then whispered, 'He's such a burden as he is right now.'

'Why don't you believe me? There's nothing easier! I'll tell you how to make him yours.'

Samar placed her head in her hands, stunned. 'It's crazy how you're thinking of this, at a time like this! Let's leave and let him sleep.' She pulled Nuzha by the hand out of the room.

'Nothing easier than nicking him!' she whispered.

'Nick him?'

Nuzha blocked the way and raised her voice. 'Yes, nick him, steal him, take him from her. If we don't think about ourselves, who will?'

'Good Lord! The way you think.'

'I mean, who is this Sahab anyway? She's got more than a few years on him, you're so much prettier and younger. Now, while he's running a fever and weak, you can take him easily.'

Disgusted, Samar shot back, 'Enough! You're so small-minded.'

'Me? Small-minded? Why? All women think like this.'

'No, not all women.'

'Okay, maybe not all, but 90 per cent of them'

Samar shot her a blistering look while she weighed the veracity of this claim. 'No, it's not possible,' she whispered. She tried to manoeuvre her way past Nuzha, but Nuzha wasn't having any of it.

'Look here, you idiot. Listen to me and you'll come out on top. At least take advantage of your being stuck here and learn something useful.'

'Me, learn something from here?' Samar smiled.

'Yes, learn something. Learn how to dress, do make-up, style your hair. Just listen to me, and I swear, he'll be like putty in your hands or a ring on your finger.'

Samar pushed her playfully. 'Okay, get out of the way and let me pass.'

'Pass where, honey? There's no way out of here. We're in the same mess together. No one's better than the other.'

'True. You're right, you're so right.' Samar shook her head sadly.

'True-true or true-false?'

'True-true.'

'We're in the same boat?'

'And there's no getting out.'

'No one's better than the other?'

'Like two sisters we are.'

'If your brothers heard you, they'd slit your throat.'

'They'd slit it.'

'And Um Sadiq would be furious.'

'She'd calm down eventually.'

'And Sitt Zakia wouldn't speak to you any more.'

'She'd come round eventually.'

Nuzha yelled, wringing her hands in frustration. 'But how come? Make me understand why!'

Samar didn't answer. She kept on looking at her, smiling patiently. 'Ah . . . '

Nuzha clapped her hands. 'You'll tell me it's because you believe in the nation, in people, right?'

'That's it,' Samar said, her smile widening.

Nuzha took her in, at once surprised and inspired. She thought to herself, *She's not shitting. She must a bit soft in the head.*

'Can I ask you for a small favour?'

Nuzha eyed her suspiciously. 'Ask me and I'll see.'

'Could I have a piece of bread and a cup of tea?'

Nuzha gasped. 'Oh God! I completely forgot.' For the first time she felt a genuine feeling of affection and rushed to the kitchen. 'Whatever is in the fridge is yours! You want a fried egg? Some soup? A glass of anise? Or even better, how about some arrack?'

Samar smiled and wagged her finger, teasing her, 'And you say that you don't care about people.'

20

He opened his eyes and saw his aunt's loving face looming. Or was it Nuzha's face? Or Samar's? He stared at the smiling eyes and the face wrapped in a white shawl.

'May the name of the Almighty protect you! Stay strong!'

'Auntie!'

'Your auntie's soul is what you are. I'm going to give you an injection and clean your wound. Tomorrow you'll be as fit as a horse.'

Horse? What horse? His friend and he had hidden in a stable and slept in the hay, among the firewood and sheep manure. Hussam had laid down, curled up on himself, like an exhausted race horse.

'If only my brother Wajih knew how gone he is!' He smiled weakly and whispered, 'Don't talk about him. Let me forget. I want to sleep.'

'Should I bring some arrack?' Nuzha interrupted.

Sitt Zakia turned and looked at her sharply, wordlessly. But Nuzha got the message and retreated. 'Okay, I'll bring him some sage tea.' The three women left the room and left the wounded to rest and sleep. When they sat in the sitting room, Sitt Zakia had a go at them. 'Why did you neglect him?'

Nuzha protested, 'Neglect him? How did we do that? From the moment he came into my house, I've been waiting on him hand and foot. If only he wasn't . . . '

'We didn't know what to do.' Samar cut her off. 'We were afraid that if we called the ambulance, he'd be found, and with the security checkpoint so close by and the curfew . . . .'

Sitt Zakia shook her head. 'Thanks be to God in any case, we only go through what He's written for us.' She looked at Nuzha in her black skirt and white blouse. 'Ah, yes, my girl, this is how you should dress,' she said with satisfaction.

Nuzha eyed her sharply and smiled mischievously. 'How's that? Correctly, you mean?'

'I mean modestly and discreetly.'

Nuzha's smile widened. 'You mean I should always dress like this?'

'My girl, is there anything better than being discreet? Praise be to God! I've got to pray my evening Isha prayer. Do you have a long skirt and a prayer mat?'

Nuzha turned to the side and mumbled, 'No, I've got a mini-skirt and tambourines.'

Samar heard her and rushed to answer, 'Anything dry and clean will do, Hajja. How about you take this towel?'

The two young women left her to perform her ablutions and pray while they went to prepare dinner. While stirring the soup, Nuzha remarked, 'Good for you! You're so patient. How do you put up with her stupidity?'

'Shame on you. There's no one sweeter than her,' Samar responded, preoccupied with chopping up the salad.

'No one sweeter than her?' Nuzha retorted as she remembered that fateful day and the cursed events that had followed. It was just an appearance that Sitt Zakia put on for people, but deep down she was just like all the others, like her nephew: white as marble on the outside but black as soot on the inside.

'We've got to be patient, Nuzha. Old women are in one river, and we're in another. But just the same they are blessings and good luck for us.'

'Blessings and good luck?' Nuzha grumbled as she kept stirring the soup. *Blessings and good luck. Hah! What blessings and good luck? After her mother's murder, were there any blessings? And other than her brother, was there any good luck? And then this old hag, the nicest of them all, what had she done to show her kindness? Saying good morning was too much for her, and now here she was in her house, occupying it, just like her nephew. And what's more, how arrogant and proud she is! Well, well! They eat your food and shit in your gob. And all their preaching, God help me! Like they say, 'If there's shit on top and shit at the bottom, it's going to smell like shit.' All they're missing are some prayer beads. Oh and Nuzha, look at how you're dressed, your make-up, your height, your hips, what a life you've suffered through! They've only got to make you wear a yanis and a baggy skirt for praying. They forget whom they're dealing with and where they're sitting! A brothel, that's what. Why don't they say it clearly? B-R-O-T-H-E-L. That's where you all are. The food that you're eating is from paying clients. Even this soup, it's brothel broth.*

Sitting at the head of the table, slurping away, Sitt Zakia commented, 'Mmmm, your soup's delicious, Nuzha. May God keep your hands safe.'

Nuzha grinned and thought, *Brothel broth Hajja, that's what you're guzzling, brothel broth.*

'Auntie Zakia, Nuzha is intelligent, a good woman,' Samar said encouragingly. 'She's got great qualities but she hasn't yet discovered them herself.'

'And who has discovered them?' Nuzha asked wryly.

'Right you are, no one's discovered them *yet*,' Samar confirmed, hopeful.

'You mean a diamond in the hands of a coal miner?' Nuzha quipped. Samar ignored Nuzha's sarcasm but she pushed on. 'A treasure in a rubbish tip?'

Sitt Zakia reprimanded her, 'Shame on you for saying such things, my girl. You're the daughter of a good family that was betrayed by time. Girls of good families have got to respect others and love them.'

Nuzha clanged her soupspoon at the bottom of the bowl and launched a tirade. 'Love people? Who loved us for us to love them? From the first day we came to this quarter, we've been under a magnifying glass. What had we done? They said that she's so young and her husband's keeling over, she's from Haifa and he's from Lud, meaning strangers without roots. And then where did she get such fair skin, blonde hair and blue eyes from? People's eyes kept spying on us until the evil eye got us and God took my father from us. And even after his death, did people leave us in peace? No. When she would sew they'd say, "Come see the blondie sew!" When she would embroider, "Come see her embroidering!" When she started playing the oud, they pulled out their hair and yelled, "Oh God, your protection! How the oud is being played in our quarter!" You all harassed her and kept on harassing her until her life became a living hell. She didn't know what she could do any more. And here you are telling me to love people. What love? Who loved me so that I could love them? Just tell me that much.'

Sitt Zakia was gobsmacked. 'Please, forgive me God.'

'Enough of your God, Mohammed and all your tosh. I'm asking you about this quarter, these people—which one of them deserves to be loved?' Nuzha yelled.

'Me, I do,' Samar calmly intervened.

Nuzha stared at her for a long time. In a serious tone, humbly, Samar said, 'Sitt Zakia, too, and feverish Hussam as well. But we're just not fully aware of it: the quarter is suffocated and our hearts are cramped. We're stuck in such a hole.'

'I swear, that's the truth. May God preserve your tongue,' Sitt Zakia affirmed, nodding her head.

'Since we're not aware, are you Nuzha the one who is?'

Confused, Nuzha looked at Samar. Such sincere words pierced her heart. *Why go and make me all emotional with your words, Samar? Isn't my sadness and bad luck enough? I've already had enough of such things.*

'And your brother Ahmed, a prince among the young men, they say a lot of good things about him. You've got every right to be proud of him and walk with your head held high,' added Sitt Zakia.

Nuzha's eyes widened. 'My brother Ahmed?'

'You too, didn't you do a spell in prison?'

'Because of a bastard,' Nuzha erupted.

'No, my girl, without such foul language. No, my darling, it's not good to say such things!'

'Your darling? Of course, of course, just like Marbout's kind of love. Show me someone who really loved me. Even the brothers of this girl sitting here who can't stop chatting and philosophizing—if I told you about them! Or even your brother Wajih, look up at that shiny crystal there, you see the bulbs? Or your nephew who, ever since coming inside this house, has been ordering me around. Me, who had cherished him so much. If you only know what he said to me and what he did.'

Sitt Zakia tried to defend her family. 'My nephew's been well raised and he only says what's right.'

'So I'm the liar, then?'

'Hush! Keep your voice down, he may wake up.'

'Yes, Nuzha, he's injured and ill, he's got to rest,' Samar chimed in.

'Let him wake up and hear me for all I care, let him wake up!' Nuzha yelled.

Sitt Zakia pleaded, 'But he's ill, and seriously wounded. What's more, he's got a fever and is in great pain. Let him rest.'

Nuzha pounded the table with her fist. 'And me? Whom can I go to find rest?' She darted to his room and stood outside the door. He opened his bloodshot eyes and let out an exhausted whisper, 'Sahab, Sahab, a drop of water, please.'

21

During the night they rebuilt the barrier. This time, it was more than a gate: it was a wall stretching from Sitt Zakia's house to Nuzha's back garden.

They brought a huge cement mixer that lit up the alley and surrounding areas with neon lights redolent of a space invasion—from afar it looked like a spaceship.

People stood peeping out from behind their windows, shutters and cracks in their curtains. When they saw the grid of bars erected and filled with tons of cement, they were certain that the wall would stand till the nation was established, or till Judgement Day itself. They didn't have the slightest inkling that it would not even last till morning, that by then it would have melted, crumbled like a stale birthday cake. But who was responsible? The least suspected people in the quarter.

The three women sat as a group discussing the grave situation at hand. Sitt Zakia complained about the long distance she had to trek whenever she wanted to go to Bab Al-Saha. The new wall didn't have a door in it; it was an impregnable block cordoning her off from her neighbours, Bab Al-Saha and the mosque.

'I don't give two craps about the mosque!' Nuzha shouted. 'I only care about the fence around my house. Why are they attacking it? This wall has got to go.'

Sitt Zakia dusted her hands off and invoked the divine power. Samar looked at her attentively and felt disappointed in herself. She was the most sensible of the three, but also the most powerless, the weakest. What would she say if they asked what she thought? That the wall being erected was an inescapable destiny? That they should just be quiet and accept their lot?

'If only Hussam were awake!' Sitt Zakia lamented.

'What would he do?' Nuzha scoffed. 'Tell me, what would he do?'

Not knowing what to do any more, Samar's eyes brimmed with tears. Samih, Hussam, Ahmed and Sadiq, where were they? The rest, the young men, where were they? Samih was a martyr, Hussam had a fever, Ahmed was a fugitive, and Sadiq, under house arrest. They all were locked up or hunted, each rendered powerless by the curfew, guard post and this wall—or, rather, this barricade.

Nuzha paced the living room, back and forth, raging like a lioness. Sitt Zakia rubbed her hands together, murmuring,

'If only he were well enough! If only!' She turned towards Samar and asked her anxiously, 'You're so quiet. Tell me, what do you think?'

Nuzha stopped pacing. She also turned to Samar, waiting for her to say something. Samar's eyes darted between the two women. Finally she stated calmly, 'I'm still thinking.'

Nuzha smiled, swiftly turned on her heel and resumed crossing the sitting room with even longer paces. Samar was mortified; such events revealed her weakness. What could she say to Nuzha now? And to Sitt Zakia? What would she say in her research? That women are weak, powerless? Or simply regurgitate Sitt Zakia's words: 'With the Intifada, nothing changed for women except more worry'? Or Nuzha's words: 'Shit and more shit on the Intifada.'

Nuzha wheeled round once more, her eyes glittering. 'Still thinking?'

Samar lowered her eyes, swallowing the sharp edge of Nuzha's knife. She turned to face Sitt Zakia again. After all, blind faith was better than indecent thoughts. Sitt Zakia's face and heart shone blessings; her hands, endowed with a love that only God could dispense. Samar got up from where she was and sat down next to the older woman. They exchanged a weary look. Sitt Zakia didn't repeat 'If only he were well enough' because she at once understood how Samar felt, the tears rolling down her cheeks. She extended her hand and pulled her into her bosom, whispering, 'It's just a passing test, my girl.' Feeling the young woman's back convulsing, she squeezed her tighter. 'No good crying, my girl. You're a blossom, a princess really!'

Samar raised her head and smiled. She wiped her tears away, regretting her moment of weakness.

'You of all girls crying?' Sitt Zakia asked incredulously. 'When they beat you, you didn't cry then, and I said to myself, "Goodness, this girl here is the bravest of men!"'

The bravest of men! She recalled the scene and what had happened: on the rooftops amid the domes stood her mother, Um Mohammed, Um Hamdallah, Fatima, Souad and other women of the quarter in their pyjamas, hair ruffled and uncovered. An unforgettable battle. That soldier who fell down into the gap, the young men's hiding place, and the attack.

'Remember? They pushed you down the stairs and you fell in front of me on the rug?'

Wiping away her tears, half-laughing, Samar confirmed, 'I remember.'

'Remember how you rubbed your neck and went back up at it?'

'How could I forget?'

'And what you said at that moment?'

'No, I don't recall that.'

Sitt Zakia looked at her, patiently and deliberately, her smile growing wider, not fading. 'I won't tell you, you should remember yourself.'

What had she said? She had completely forgotten. In this and that, God be praised, there was still a kernel of awareness in her brain.

'No, I don't remember, but I understand what you're getting at.'

And, in less then an hour, the operation was planned out, down to the most minute detail.

22

Sitt Zakia asked for the garden hose. Over the flames of the fire, they heated some metal kebab skewers and pierced twenty holes in the hose. Nuzha brought a sack of sugar that Samar, under the cover of night, had transported to the rooftop. The two of them poured the sugar into a basin of water and stirred it. When they had finished, Sitt Zakia said, 'If they stop me, I have my pass.'

Without further delay, she slipped out from Nuzha's back garden. Once on her own roof, she pulled the hose and positioned it onto the fresh cement. With the tap open, the water seeped through, infiltrating the cement, steadily dissolving it, breaking it down.

In the morning, the alley woke to the sound of hammering. From behind the glass of their windows and the slats of their shutters, the neighbours saw two bars of iron: one hanging from Sitt Zakia's house and the other from Nuzha's garden. With each hammer blow, the cement crumbled like bran. Within minutes, only a skeleton of bars remained of the barrier.

Children streamed out onto the street, pushing against what was left of the wall until it fell over. The entire quarter resounded with the women's ululations.

A woman standing by her window on the first floor with a tub of butter in hand yelled out, her voice sonorous, 'Repeat children, repeat after me:

They've knocked down the wall
Knocked it down.
And the country's free
They've lifted her up.
Come on, children
Let's celebrate!
The state is the bride
Celebrate her wedding!

The children danced on the rubble; the windows of the quarter opened up despite the curfew; women threw sugared almonds and nougat; the children gobbled them up, shrieking. A raging joy swept through the street. Raindrops started to fall but the drumbeats didn't relent. Despite the thunder and roar of the wind, the children kept singing, louder and louder. The thunder rolled and rumbled, pipes in the quarter burst, water streamed forth, gushing, sweeping away the cement and dirt on the street.

The children wandered aimlessly, stretching their hands out to the sky, chanting noisily, possessed.

We've knocked down the wall
Knocked it down
And the country's free
We've lifted her up.
C'mon you all, let's celebrate!
The state has risen
By our own hands!

23

When the army discovered what had happened, they started another round of searching. By definition, it wasn't a search but, rather, organized mass revenge. They rounded up all the males, from the young to the elderly. They made them stand in the square, their faces ground into the wall, hands raised above their heads all day long. In the meantime, they rebuilt the wall with enormous rocks.

They brought the rocks over in diggers and blocked off the mouth of the alley with monstrous boulders. Only a cat could squeeze its way through. When they had finished, they announced the end of the curfew. People spilt into the square and Khan Al-Tujjar, as many as you would expect on Judgement Day itself, rushing to restock their depleted larders, including that which the soldiers had destroyed.

They returned home just as swiftly, groceries in hand, before unrest broke out.

In the morning, when the hour hand had scarcely brushed ten, all hell broke loose. And by one in the afternoon Nablus went back to what it had always been: a ghost town.

24

When the curfew was lifted, Samar slipped out from Nuzha's back door and returned home, anxious about how her family would respond to her prolonged absence. What would she say if they asked: Where were you? Where did you sleep? What did you eat? What did you drink? Would she say that she had been at Nuzha's? Her brothers would slaughter her without a second thought. She was in no position to confront or challenge them. Everyone was suppressed, on edge, their nerves fraught, frailer than straw. Chaos welcomed her: a broken sideboard, shattered glass from the dining table strewn atop another table abutting it, which was itself leaning against a chair. Dishes in pieces, smashed glasses and other things thrown in a crate that had taken the place of the rubbish bin.

Samar heard the clanging of pots and pans. Going into the kitchen, she saw her mother in front of the sink washing the dishes. Her mother was balanced on one leg, giving the raised one a rest. Samar felt a wave of guilt wash over her as she remembered how she had left her mother alone all this time to fend for herself with the relentless housework. Her brothers never lifted a finger unless it was to stretch their hands out for food or to pick up a queen of hearts. How many times she had told them off but it was pointless. One of them would be disgruntled, and another would make fun of her, turning the whole thing into a joke that inevitably ended with her leaving them and hiding out on the roof behind the domes. There, she would read, think and try to understand reality to a deeper degree. She wasn't a child any more; the things that used to irk her back then became a link in the chain of civilization: history, progress of nations, gender, depletion and a complex oppression that assumed three forms, not one. And as the daughter of a baker, she had to submit to all three. How heavy her burden was!

Her mother turned round to see Samar in the doorway and gasped. She raised her hand full of lather and rattled in a hoarse voice, 'Now you decide to show your face? Damn you!'

The more Samar tried to calm her mother down, the louder her cries became. From one word to the next, Samar pieced together what had happened in her absence: they had stormed the house and taken her brothers who happened to be home at the time; only Sadiq and Umar remained now. After staccato panting, a patchy description of events, curses and threats, the interrogation began: 'Where were you during the curfew? NINE DAYS! May God punish you, NINE

DAYS! You could have called, sent someone, written a note, jumped between the roofs, done something, anything, but not be missing all this time. What will your brothers say? Oh what bad luck I have! What will people say? Such a scandal! I swear they're going to slit your throat. Our soot and humiliation aren't enough for you? Our tears and distress aren't enough for you? That we should worry about you, too? Aren't we miserable enough? May God punish you! What do I tell your brothers when they ask? What do I tell Sadiq? And Umar?'

Finally Samar was forced to confess and told her mother what happened from the knocking on Nuzha's door to her farewell.

The woman started slapping her face. 'May you be cursed! Nuzha wasn't enough, eh? Hussam as well! Blackest of scandals this is. You were with the nephew in the same house? Under one roof? And in which house? Sakina's. Is this how you want your life to end, baker's daughter? Don't you understand this means the end? It will be the end, your living hell. You, who we always used to say was the reasonable one, the educated one, a good head on your shoulders. But you turned out to be an empty nut, the shell is there all right, thick and strong, but knock, knock, knock, nobody's home!'

Slapping her cheeks, she collapsed on a chair, moaning. Samar retreated to her secret kingdom, her usual hideaway full of daydreams and ideas. Her mother kept on gasping, moaning, shrieking, complaining. She ended the scene by

having an anxiety attack; she lay on the sofa and declared that
her hour had come.

25

Samar went to her bed and hid under the covers, shaking
with fear and anger. Angry at herself because she was scared,
and scared of her fear because she realized that she was still
floundering in the middle of this closed ring of knotted complex familial relationships. Here, in this house, she felt like
an infinitesimal insect caught in a spider's web, no more.
Where were her ideas and theories? All of them fell to pieces
in front of a gasp, a word, an insinuation. Everything ended
with a 'Shame on you!' Countless times she tried to discuss
the matter but then withdrew. She became the butt of their
jokes whenever her brothers would get together to play
cards. She'd say 'Oppression' and they'd say 'Press the dough'.
She'd talk of travels by 'bicycle' and they'd retort, 'Riding a
woman is the best kind of ride.' She'd talk of how the army
was wiping out neighbourhoods, and they'd reply, 'Is a bare
face—wiped clean—any good to look at?'

She ran away from all this to university, then to the association, then scientific research. How heavy her burden was!
The more she understood things, the more they weighed on
her and the more she feared. Today, she knew that change
wouldn't come with the establishment of the state. Political
matters were a different animal altogether from morals,

religion and aesthetics. Political matters could be settled, whereas customs, women . . . 'The road is long, my sisters,' she had explained at an association meeting. 'The road is long and hard.' Much younger girls smoking Kent and wearing leather jackets had shouted back, 'No! The road is the one we're walking right now!' They were the daughters of lawyers, doctors, mayors and traders, who had come from London and New York for the summer. In broken Arabic, they spoke gibberish, calling women 'Mizz' and men 'chauvinists'. When Samar had said 'The road is long,' they had yelled in drawn out voices, 'But the road is here and we're on it!'

Here? In the alley? Or here in the Al-Qaryon quarter? Or in Al-Yasmina and Khan Al-Tujjar? Here, in front of the place for ablutions at the mosque in Bab Al-Saha in the middle of town? But even the ugliest of them wouldn't stay committed to such comments in front of the cafe or the bakery. What would her brother Sadiq say at the bakery? With profound belief he'd say, 'These girls are really suffering, they've got no one to guide them. Send them to me, behind the shop, and I promise you I'll take care of them.'

And the occupation? The organization? Which organization? Her brothers had said, 'Take care of Mum and the association. If you want, you can do two research studies instead of one, but on the condition that you don't go out, don't protest, not here, not there. We five, each of us is worth ten men. We, who defend and fight for the country. You, keep quiet, sit down and have a rest.'

She was in a world where it was impossible to have a rest, keep quiet or distract herself. She had to be patient, to better understand things and accept the bitterness of life before arriving at love and faith. Whenever her brothers made fun of her, she'd keep silent, smile, remain indifferent. Why should she get riled up? She had a world of her own that they couldn't get their grubby hands on. She had her mind, her burdens, the patience of a camel, and skin as thick as a crocodile or, better yet, a turtle shell. This was her reality, no more, no less.

But reality changes. Sometimes she wouldn't walk straight but leap like a cat. The Intifada shook the dust off of them, shook the earth without warning. Brothers told their sisters, 'No demonstrations.' They were surprised then when the demonstrations reached women in the depths of their houses. 'No going out or making a spectacle of yourself.' The spectacles reached their bedrooms, the women in their pyjamas, hair undone: fist-fighting, yelling, cursing, attacking the intruding soldiers. 'Other than our country, we don't have any religion.' They spontaneously went out on the streets— revolution had become their religion. Sleep was out of the question.

Golden days like those of a birthday. In a revolution, one is born a hundred times and dies a thousand more. The revolution isn't a rocket but a river that flows and pours forth. Sometimes foreign aid sinks, rain becomes scarce, the river goes through difficult times, drying up, seeming as fine as a silk thread. Other times it breaks forth, like a turbulent volcano, sweeping away all in its path, deafening. Oh generous sky, oh angry earth, anger that, like a storm, chooses its hour. Then the cycle comes to an end and goes back to how it was: the river becomes an oscillating thread again, the revolution returns to reality, the boulder tumbles back to the bottom of the river and Sisyphus picks up his load once more.

26

A hand shook her awake. Shouting. Then slaps. 'Where were you?'

Her mother pulled him back and yelled, 'She was doing work, leave her!'

'What work? For NINE days?'

He began to beat her mindlessly, her face, her head, her back. 'You slut. You want to be like Nuzha, do you? I swear I'll slit your throat.'

She didn't cry out, sob, open her mouth to breath a word or resist. When the soldiers had hit her, she had fought back, bringing down the wooden plank in her hand on them, and anything she could find to strike them with. But now, she was just a dingy tossed by the waves and squalls. An overwhelming feeling of shame, being completely crushed, being worthless and insignificant, pushed her down. She was disgusted by everything: by him, her mother, her younger brother standing in the doorway watching, not lifting a finger to object or saying a word. How easily he had forgotten their shared secrets. She would give him her books to read, knit things for him to wear, help him translate his texts. Her younger brother watched on while her older brother flexed his muscles. When he finally took leave of her, she was completely wrecked: hair tangled, temples swollen, black and blue all over, her head swimming, spots floating and fading before her eyes. At the sudden call to prayer she felt dead. Not the occupation, nor the army, not all the demons on earth could grind her to a pulp in this fashion. She was overcome with stupefaction, by a desire to run to the furthest point possible, far from her family and all the pettiness of this world. She left her bedroom and heard them in the sitting room watching the news. She climbed the steps to the roof and saw the city engulfed in darkness, some lights here and there. The cold was biting despite the starry sky, pure and twinkling; she heard the echo of loudspeakers saluting the city's resistance, the destruction of the barrier and the wall. At this moment in time, the destruction of the wall seemed like an old song, an old film, images torn from a dream. Destroying the wall, the cement, that proud feeling of accomplishment, the memory of Nuzha, Sitt Zakia and the injured young man: all that now seemed far away, like a wish. She was only left with astonishment and the pain of falling back down to rock-hard earth.

She surveyed the city foggily, closed her eyes and almost fell. She leant against the low boundary wall to regain her balance. From where she was, she saw the new barrier, titanic boulders blocking the way.

27

Nuzha sat on the ground, leaning against Hussam's bed and watching Sitt Zakia, who sat cross-legged, bubbling away on her hookah, and remembered her grandmother Um Abdallah in Seilat Al-Zahar. She would sit them down round the fire, grilling carrots and potatoes, telling stories: Sitt Al-Hasn, the beauty queen, who spun wool so well; her father the ogre, who was fattening her up to wolf her down on her wedding night. That wasn't even the best story. There was Derbissa the orphan, who lost her brother and lived out the rest of her life weeping and wailing. Derbissa the beautiful, with her soft hair and moon-like face, who would sing in such a melancholy voice that it made all the girls cry. Nuzha would cry, too, and tell her grandmother, while burying her face in her lap that smelt like bread and the clay oven, 'Why granny? *Haram.* It's so unfair.' Derbissa's brother had disappeared and left her to die of misery. *Oh Ahmed, where are you?* Nuzha wiped her tears with the corner of her sleeve and sighed in silence.

Sitt Zakia looked at her with interest and stopped sucking on her hookah pipe. *Your wisdom and pardon, O Most*

Merciful One. Praise be to God, how had it never crossed my mind that this girl was all alone, that in her loneliness, she cried, was afraid and suffered! Wasn't she also made of flesh and blood? Was it because she was Sakina's daughter? Or because she was a daughter of this scandalous house? And Sakina herself, what did she do? Um Mohammed, Um Hamdallah and Um Sadiq all had a clear and decisive answer on the matter. But it never sat well with me, ever since that cursed girl had thrown out the questions like: How can we be precise? How can we confirm? Where's the proof? In scientific research . . . scientific, scientific . . . only God knows all, my girl, and we only receive what he has destined for us. Sakina is dead and that was her fate; Nuzha lives on and will meet her fate, too. But I'm more worried about you Samar, my girl, you're so young.

'Nuzha.'

Nuzha raised her head and looked at Sitt Zakia.

'Come here, my girl. Come next to me.'

She hesitated, weighing up how sincere the old lady was being. Sitt Zakia held out her hand, insisting, 'Come, come.'

Nuzha crawled over. She buried her face in Sitt Zakia's lap and broke down. 'I'm all alone, Hajja, all alone.'

Sitt Zakia placed her hand on the young girl's head and recited a quick prayer, 'Lead us down the straight path, the path of those you have blessed, those who you are not angry with, who have not gone astray. Ameen.'

Hussam opened his eyes—heavy with fatigue—with difficulty, taking in the strange scene before him. His heart fluttered. But he was still feverish, in pain. The khaki uniforms … he sunk down into a bottomless stormy sea, his back drenched in sweat.

'As soon as he came inside, it felt like Ahmed had come back to take me away with him, away from this quarter, this house, these people and their insults,' Nuzha said. 'But obviously, I was wrong. Always wrong. I'm like that, rely too much on my imagination. If only God would call me back to him, then I'd finally get some peace! What keeps me here? I've got no backbone and my heart is too soft. But if I really was strong enough, I would have done myself in and been at peace.'

'No, my girl,' said Sitt Zakia, soothing her and rubbing her back. 'Don't say such things. Don't be ungrateful for the blessings you have. You're still young and beautiful, and tomorrow is full of good things for you.'

Nuzha began to whimper. 'G-good things?' *Good things, hah!* Nuzha thought to herself, *Damn you, Marbout. Sitting on your rocking chair in your palace up high in the mountains, with your wife as black as a crow, who's only missing a beak. You've got to open your eyes, you blind bat, after all it's not a nose that she has but a beak.*

* * *

Marbout, was sprawled out in the satin bedsheets. He started to scream with laughter. Nuzha, in front of the mirror, was imitating his wife. 'She walks like this, raises her left eyebrow like that while she gabs on and wriggles in front of the salesman.'

* * *

Marbout's wife examined the piece of cloth from top to bottom. She felt the fabric, turning the folds and seams inside out, checking the brand, before she asked anxiously, 'You sure it's French? Sure it's come from Paris?'

'Yes, Yes. You just feel the fabric. Look here, look here . . . see the texture? The wool comes from Kashmir but the design is Christian Dior. Because of the taxes and the situation in the country right now, the labels were taken off. Just yesterday the merchandise came from the port. Chic styles, the latest! There's only two of each piece.'

She raised her turned-up nose even higher, offended, to the point of getting angry. 'There should only be one of each piece, no more.'

He removed the suit from the hanger with exaggerated reverence. 'Okay, I've heard you. Next time, there will only be one of each piece, and that's it. Look at these buttons, the cut, only worthy of people who deserve to wear it, worthy of your beautiful shoulders, worthy of someone elegant like you.'

* * *

'When she came out of the fitting room wearing the suit, and saw me coming out of the opposite one in the exact same outfit, her eyes froze. Her nostrils flared up and she rushed back into the fitting room immediately.'

After hearing Nuzha's tale, Marbout started laughing even more raucously and nearly pissed all over the red satin sheets.

* * *

Whenever she was with him she'd soar above the cotton-ball clouds, above the tiled rooftops, the pine trees, entire forests. Then he threw her away and she tumbled down, down, while he stayed on his rocking chair up high.

'If I really was strong enough, I would have done myself in and been at peace.'

'No, my girl, ask for God's forgiveness, why blaspheme like this?'

'I wish Ahmed would come home, even for just an hour . . . .'

'Maybe the poor fellow is hidden in a cellar or a cave somewhere. God strengthen him, protect him, all of them.'

'He can't even come here for one hour?'

'How long has it been since he's been back?'

'Since the day he left.'

'And when did he leave?'

'He left when the Intifada started and never came back. So many times, I've seen masked men in the alley and told myself, *maybe* that's him. But it never is. When my mum was murdered, I saw a masked man in the alley, and ran behind him, calling out, "Ahmed, Ahmed!" He turned round and said, "I'm not Ahmed." But it *was* him. Why would he lie?'

Sitt Zakia nodded her head in silence, not making any comments. Her eyes met the red ones of her nephew. She patted the young girl's back and whispered, 'Hussam's awake. Give us some space.'

He closed his eyes again and sank into the sea of salt. His body felt light, as light as an ostrich feather. He fluttered along, flew, blew across balconies, above the town squares, the domes of the bakery and the mosque. The mosque had a beautiful place for ablutions: marble tiles, tulip patches and a sagebrush with feathery, dust-coloured foliage, nicknamed 'the Prophet's grey hair'. Particularly effective against kidney stones and incontinence. The sheikh would boil it and drink it but to no avail. He still suffered from renal colic and, on top of that, a loose bladder. Ahmed teased him once, 'If I were in your shoes, I wouldn't drink it.'

The sheikh eyeballed him, glaring. 'If I were in your shoes . . . just forget it, you already know.' He walked down the stone hallway, gliding on top of the marble tiles, his jibba puffing up like a sail.

Ahmed sat on the steps, his chin resting in his palm, lost in an abyss of thought. 'What's wrong Ahmed?'

'Nothing.'

'Man, what's wrong?'

'Don't ask.'

'Hero, just tell me already.'

Ahmed turned his upper torso, chin still nestled in his palm, and repeated, 'If I were a real hero, if I were a real . . .' Then he sunk back into the sea of salt.

'How old is he?' Sitt Zakia inquired.

'Barely seventeen.'

'Maybe he doesn't know.

'How can he not? Even my older brother Muawiya heard what happened and wrote to me.'

'He wrote you a letter?'

'And called me and told me to come.'

'Why didn't you go?'

'Ahmed? And the house?

The two women fell silent and the older one went back to gurgling the hookah. *If I had been her, I would have escaped. What's keeping her here? She's waiting for Ahmed to come back here? Poor thing doesn't realize that maybe, just maybe he does know? Only God knows!*

Nuzha stood in front of the window, looking through the glass. The leaves of the lemon tree were dancing, glittering in the rain; sprouts of green were coming through the dried-out brown grass; a sparrow the size of a butterfly hovered over the daffodils and lilies of the valley; the fence enclosing the back garden was as it always had been: ancient, solid, high, blanketed with moss and ferns. She remembered days from long ago when fairy lights would be hanging from posts and branches. Muawiya and his gang would spend the night under the foliage. That's her last image of him: the leaves, the poles, the wires stretched between the branches . . . but without the lights. Whatever she had felt for him, there was only a grain left. Why had he asked how she was? Well, he hadn't asked at all, really, and neither had she. He hadn't written a letter or picked up the phone. Why had she lied? Just like that, she didn't know. She liked the idea of America, and the idea of an exiled brother taking the time to send her a letter, or call her—she liked that. And Asim—that shit—if only he'd take the time to write or ask how she was doing. If only . . . but he never did.

She sighed. 'If only Ahmed came back, we would leave together. America's big and there are so many people, nobody knows or asks about the other. There, we can get lost in the crowd. Muawiya and me, we'll work in a restaurant and Ahmed will study to become a doctor. I'll work myself to the bone for him. Um Hassan's daughter put her brothers through medical school. Me too, I'll do the same for Ahmed.'

'You speak English?'

'I'll pick it up.'

Sitt Zakia shook her head sadly.

'Why are you shaking your head, Hajja? I'll learn it lickety-split. I learnt Hebrew in the blink of an eye.'

'So you speak Hebrew?'

'Better than a nightingale.'

'Shush. Lower your voice. He might hear you.'

'He's still sleeping.'

'Maybe he'll wake up.'

'And so what? Everyone speaks Hebrew like a nightingale. You know what, Hajja? Hebrew is even easier than Arabic.'

'And English?'

'I know a couple of words, not a lot.'

'And Ahmed?'

'Not a word.'

Sitt Zakia shook her head wordlessly. She went back to sucking her hookah pipe and looking pensive.

'America is seductive. Tell me, have you seen the American TV show *Love Boat*? I can't wait for the next episode. Asim, shit that he is, went to America and rode the *Love Boat*, the actual yacht from the soap opera. He told me it's just like it is on TV. He promised to take me but he never did. How I hope God ends his life. O God, by your love for our Prophet, Jesus, Moses, Sheikh Al-Imad, call Asim back to you and help me get my revenge.'

'No my dear, it's not good to curse others so.'

'Are you going to keep on telling me what's good and what's bad?'

'Keep your voice down.'

'I heard you the first time.'

They both fell silent. A memory came to Sitt Zakia and she smiled. 'Back when I worked at the hospital, I learnt a few words of English and started babbling: *yes, no, thank you very much.*'

A rattle of a laugh escaped from Nuzha's lips; Sitt Zakia hit her with her hookah pipe. She stifled her own laughter behind her hands and started snorting instead. Sitt Zakia kept on smiling, restraining her guffaws which threatened to escape despite herself.

Wiping tears from her eyes, Nuzha said, 'I know a whole lot more than that. Once, Asim brought a journalist with him and I started speaking English with him, and he understood me.'

'But how, if you only know a couple of words?'

'I tricked him.'

'You tricked him?'

'I made some gestures, moved my hands, moved my eyes up and down. Asim laughed and said, 'Again.'

'And the Ingleezi?'

'He was American, not English.'

'And the Amreeki?'

'He told me, "Good job." '

Sitt Zakia opened her eyes, the pipe hanging between her chin and her lips, then she slowly said, 'He said it in Arabic?'

'No, in English.'

'How do you say it in English?'

'What, you don't believe me?'

Sitt Zakia didn't respond, so Nuzha backtracked. 'Okay, okay. He didn't say it with all the letters but I understood it off the cuff.'

'So then, what did he say?'

'He said many things.'

'How do you know that he understood you?'

'You won't get angry with me if I tell you?'

'Why would I get angry?'

'Okay, I'll tell you. When I tricked him, he looked at me: mouth wide open, like an idiot, while Asim laughed. Then he grabbed my hand and kissed it here.'

Sitt Zakia was silent, the hookah pipe forgotten against her chin. Nuzha looked out of the corner of her eye and said, trying to reconnect the broken line of affection, 'The problem isn't the English or American man, Hajja. The problem is Ahmed and how he is not here. If only he'd come back, we could make a run for it!'

Irritated, Sitt Zakia snapped. 'Stay at home, be discreet and stop talking about America. Enough of your childishness. Who told you he wants to travel in the first place?'

'Oh, he wants to. That's for sure. Before running off, he wanted to travel far away. Sometimes, he would come home from school and start crying about it. But Mum didn't want to. She would say, "How can we live abroad? We're just women and Ahmed is still so young." But now things have changed. My mother's gone, Ahmed's grown up and become a man.'

'How's he a man? He's still a child.'

Hussam twisted in his bed and opened his bloodshot eyes.

Nuzha insisted, 'No, he's not a child. Seventeen is not a child. A young man fighting in the Intifada isn't a child. America has got it all—it's heaven compared to here. Ahmed's just got to be smart and become a doctor. My sweat and tears will put him through school. I wish he would just come back and speak to me! If he comes today, we can leave tomorrow.' Nuzha turned round and stuck her forehead to the window, breathing heavily and fogging up the glass. She remembered things, so many things. Things that seemed bizarre now, even impossible, or disgusting. How did it all happen? It all swirled round in her head: the scenes, the faces, the disgust! Ahmed would be hidden in a corner next to the jasmine planter under the lemon tree behind the house. Ahmed the child, with no friends, who couldn't play in the streets. And yet, he'd look into her eyes steadily for some time and insist, 'Asim's going to take us with him, right?'

'Right.'

'And we're going to ride the *Love Boat*, right?'

'Sure, sure.'

'And we'll see Michael Jackson, Madonna and *Dallas* the show?'

'Yes, yes.' But there was a surprise in store for her. Instead of riding the *Love Boat*, she found herself in the women's section of Ramla prison. And instead of Madonna and *Dallas*, she was lost amid a sea of Israeli criminals and Arab activists. She wasn't a Jewish prostitute or an Arab activist. Whenever she passed by, some of them winked at her and others whispered. Finally, an Arab woman took pity on her and said plainly, 'He really got you, didn't he? You poor idiot.'

'No, he wouldn't do this to me, he loves me, he adores me. It's his wife that's ugly and difficult. He's going to make me his wife!' They fought and she was thrown into solitary confinement.

'He made a fool of you,' a Jewish prostitute told her, then another, and another, then all the Arab women activists and the Israeli prostitutes, even the walls, and the bars, even the investigating officer and the prison guard—but she didn't utter a word. Why did they beat her, and not Asim? Why did they kill her mother, and not Asim? How was he able to distance himself from everything, just like Ahmed did, only to disappear, melt into thin air and never come back? She begged for mercy, waited for death, willing it to come, hoping that Ahmed would return. She sighed for the umpteenth time and murmured, 'I just want to see him, just for an hour! If he came today, we would be off tomorrow.'

'Where would you go?' asked Sitt Zakia sadly. 'To the end of the world? To other people's countries? You're a woman now and he's still so young.'

'He's not young.'

Hussam moved in his bed and whispered, 'No, he's not young.'

'You're awake?' Sitt Zakia exclaimed.

'You see? You see?' Nuzha rushed to say. 'Even Hussam says that he's not young.'

He opened his red eyes and said slowly, 'Nuzha, Ahmed's become a man.' He fixed his eyes on her and said with a tenderness that she hadn't ever known, 'And he won't go abroad.'

She stood transfixed, still like a statue, eyeing Hussam's face for a long time. He turned his gaze towards the light coming in from the windowpanes and the bars. He said with calculated gentleness, 'And neither will you, Nuzha.'

28

Nuzha came bounding down the stairs from the roof, yelling, 'Hajja, Hajja, you've got guests!' Sitt Zakia came out of the bathroom, her hands dripping from performing ablutions. She asked about the guests and Nuzha let her know that all she saw was a woman in a long black coat, whose head was wrapped in a grey shawl, sitting on the doorstep of Sitt Zakia's house. Who was she? She didn't know. How long had she been sitting there? Nuzha didn't know that either. Was she pregnant? Her coat, fastened to the last button, didn't show a protruding belly. Sitt Zakia didn't seem too concerned. Staying by the bedside of her injured nephew was more important than all the pregnant women in the quarter. These women had the whole quarter for themselves, in any case. Hussam, though, was being chased and didn't have anyone by his side except for her and God and . . . Nuzha.

She prayed the noon prayer, then later, the afternoon prayer, and shortly before the sunset prayer, they both heard footsteps in the alley by the back garden. They were frightened. Sitt Zakia rushed to Hussam's room to hide while Nuzha peeked out through the crack of the closed window. She saw Samar accompanying the woman in the grey shawl and black coat. She opened the metal door. A gust rushed in, sharp as a sword; the baubles of the crystal chandelier clashed against one another. Samar whispered as she closed the door, 'It's Um Azzam, I met her on the doorstep.'

Nuzha swallowed a gasp, backing away from the door. The lady stretched out her hand, greeting her without a word, and plopped down on the first sofa she came across to rest after having climbed the stairs. She was still panting. Her swollen eyes were lowered, her weary face was puffy, her veins straining against her skin.

Samar's eyes darted between the hostess and the guest. 'Um Azzam has come to see Sitt Zakia, but Sitt Zakia isn't at home. I told her maybe she's at the neighbour's. Our neighbour is at full term, ready to give birth.'

In a heartbeat, Nuzha caught on and responded swiftly, 'Ah, yes! Sitt Zakia is here but the woman hasn't popped yet. Wait a bit, and I'll call her.' She walked briskly into Hussam's room and closed the door behind her. 'It's your sister-in-law,' she said in a low voice.

Sitt Zakia's eyes opened wide in surprise. 'My sister-in-law? What's she doing here at this time of the evening?'

Nuzha bit her lower lip. Sitt Zakia looked from Nuzha to the injured young man. She asked, 'Does she know?'

Nuzha made a moue.

Um Azzam's gaze swept over every corner in the house. 'Goodness, this house is big, but a bit stuffy. Why are all the windows shut? Can you open one so we can breathe?' She started fanning herself with her hand, breathing heavily. Samar opened a window. The crystal beads swayed in the wind as they crashed into one another. Um Azzam raised her eyes and remarked, dumbfounded, 'Why, this chandelier is just like the one I have!'

Samar nodded without saying anything. Silence blanketed the room once more, the atmosphere suffocating.

Sitt Zakia came out ensconced in white: in a long skirt and a yanis. She had been preparing herself to pray. 'Welcome! What a surprise!' The two women exchanged kisses and sat on the sofa. Only their breathing could be heard. Sitt Zakia was waiting for Um Azzam's reaction to know how she should behave: she appeared distracted, slow, stupid even. After having observed her enough, she asked Um Azzam anxiously, 'Is Wajih well?'

'He's well,' she answered briefly, her eyes fixed on an undetermined spot on the ground.

'And Hussam?'

The woman shook her head but kept silent.

Sitt Zakia looked over to the two young women and asked, 'Which of you would like to make us some tea?'

They both scurried off to the kitchen.

Sitt Zakia turned to Um Azzam and asked with concern, 'What's wrong, Um Azzam? Everything well, I hope?'

The woman placed her hand on her head, then waved it round in the air, sobbing. 'My head's going to explode.'

'It will be fine. I hope to God it's nothing serious.'

Um Azzam didn't respond. She turned her face in the other direction and talked over her shoulder. 'Hajja, I've come here and I won't go back.'

Sitt Zakia started; this was the last thing she had expected. *Abu Azzam is a good-for-nothing, yes. Her eldest child Azzam took his Green Card and married an American girl, yes. Abu Azzam's brothers, who were abroad, have demanded their portion of the rent, yes. They have had their arguments, come to blows, things have been broken, yes, yes. But this 'I've come here and I won't go back' is something I have never expected. Why now, sister? Haven't you endured this your whole life and never complained? You've been discreet and reasonable for so long. After all these years, now with white hair, now you let your neighbours hear your fights? There is no power or strength save in God . . .*

The woman turned back around and stretched out her dry, chapped hands to Sitt Zakia, raising her heavy eyes for the first time, pleading in an extremely humble tone, 'Please take me in.'

What? Sitt Zakia opened her eyes wide. 'What's wrong with you?' she whispered.

Um Azzam took Sitt Zakia's hands in hers and felt the roughness of wood against her skin. 'I beg you, my children have upped and left me. My brothers are abroad, they don't ask after me. I only have God and you. I'll be your servant: cook your food for you and carry your bag from house to house.'

As if stung, Sitt Zakia wrenched her hands back. 'God forgive me, God forgive me. What are you saying, poor woman? Calm down and depend on God!'

Um Azzam took in a breath as fine as a kebab skewer and moaned, 'I can't take any more, Hajja. I've had enough. Your brother has destroyed me, driven me mad.'

Sitt Zakia's eyes moved away. She murmured, 'What a pity for women!' Then she remembered her brother, his intense eyes, bulging veins, how red he got when he was angry, the way he would splutter. She grew scared and sought protection from the All-Merciful, and asked worriedly, 'Does Wajih know?'

'Whether he knows or not, I'm not moving from here.'

'But this is a neighbour's house.'

Um Azzam shook her head stubbornly. 'I'll go wherever you go.'

Sitt Zakia thought on her feet. *If only she knew this was Sakina's house! What would she do then?* 'But you know whose house this is, right?' she asked cautiously.

Um Azzam shook her head like a stubborn schoolgirl. 'Whoever it belongs to, where you go, I go.'

Sitt Zakia insisted, 'But do you *know* whose house this is?'

'Whose can it be? Abid Azzatti the gypsy? Azrael, the angel of death? Even if it were your brother's, I wouldn't go back.'

Sitt Zakia's ploy had failed. She turned around looking for help. She saw Nuzha standing at the kitchen door, with the tea tray in hand. Nuzha smiled and whispered wickedly, 'Welcome, Wajih's wife.'

29

The three women agreed that Um Azzam was suffering a nervous breakdown. The absence of her children, compounded by her husband's brutality and the circumstances of the Intifada, had gnawed away at her nerves. She was in a situation that no one would want to be in. As such, they concluded that if she saw her son in his current state, her condition would deteriorate even further and he would encourage her to stay away from her home.

Guilefully, Nuzha commented that she had no objection to hosting Wajih's wife for as long as she lived, because 'My home is your home.' Sitt Zakia knitted her eyebrows and pursed her lips. At the end of the day, Um Azzam was her brother's wife and her brother's reputation was the priority here. Whatever mistakes he had made, he was still a respectable man with a social position to maintain. What would people say if they heard that his wife was staying in Sakina's house? God forbid! And what about herself? What would people say if they learnt that Sitt Zakia was in Sakina's house? Probably nothing. Not only was she from this quarter but, because of her old age, no one would be suspicious of her motives. Fine, then. And what of Hussam? Hussam was a man and nothing could tarnish his reputation. What would they say if they heard that Hussam had slept with Nuzha, the same Nuzha who had slept with an army of men? They'd say what they wanted. Who among them hadn't done it? Which of them hadn't frequented this house? They entered it whenever they wished, from the first to the last, they were men and no one would ever reproach them. But what about women, her sister-in-law, Samar? Protect us, O God. Why hadn't she warned the girl more vehemently not to come to Sakina's? Wasn't she younger than Um Azzam? Wasn't she more beautiful than her? Wasn't she a respectable young girl even if she was the baker's daughter?

She said to the two young women that she would try to convince Um Azzam to reconsider her decision and go back home to her husband. Also, she wouldn't bring up Hussam. In order for her to be able to achieve this mission, they would have to give her some space, so that she could be frank and talk with ease. After all, Hussam shouldn't be left alone. If they two sat with him, then she could focus on convincing his mother to get her head straight.

And like that they split up, the young women together and the older women together: Hussam's mother and Sitt Zakia in the sitting room, Samar and Nuzha in Hussam's room.

Sitting cross-legged on the prayer mat, Sitt Zakia said, 'Calm down and depend on God, Um Azzam.'

The woman raised her head and responded piously, 'There is no god but God.'

Sitt Zakia clasped her prayer beads and started worrying them. 'Allah, Mohammed, Essa, Musa. Allah, Mohammed, Allah, Mohammed.' She stopped abruptly and cleared her throat. 'My opinion is—and now don't get upset with me, Um Azzam—that you should go back to your house and be a decent wife. Don't blame me for this, but people like us, women, we only feel at ease in our own homes. Your whole life you've been so patient and discreet. And after all this time, after your boys have become men, you leave your home, Um Azzam?'

Um Azzam looked at her through her swollen eyelids and didn't answer. She was weighing the truth of her words and saw that what Sitt Zakia had said hit the nail on the head. Does a woman have any other kingdom other than her house? Does she have a crown for her head other than her husband? But how to go back to him after he's raised his hand against her? Years had passed, long years, maybe since Hussam's birth, since he had last hit her and she had come to forget what a thrashing tasted like. She would hear about so and so being beaten up and she would scoff, with her nose in the air, 'What a world! Are there still women like that?' She would turn her face away from battered women and forget their plight altogether.

But any time she was invited out somewhere, she would look on enviously at the women dressed in the latest fashions.

She was Sa'adi Al Jallab's daughter, after all—the biggest trader in the north. She had left her father's house as the focus of a grand, opulent wedding jamboree that stretched from Khaduri University to the outskirts of Wadi Touffah. Anyone who was anyone had been there, amid the cars and ululations. Her wedding gown, in fact, her whole trousseau had been imported from Beirut. She had been elegant, pampered, beautiful, a beauty queen really, and she had swum gleefully in her good fortune. But what was left now? She wasn't pretty, wasn't young, wasn't under her father's protection. Her father had died broken, humiliated. Her brothers had emigrated after selling their plots of land. Her boys had grown up and left her behind. The eldest was settled in America and the youngest was being hunted like the other young men.

'Poor woman! It's as if you never had children!' That's what Wajih would repeat like a broken record. 'Your eldest is a deadbeat who doesn't even care how you're doing and the other is a vagabond.'

The first time he had said all this, she kicked up a fuss. 'My children? *My* children? Shame on you! Wash your mouth, Abu Azzam.'

He spat and exploded, 'Wash my mouth, eh? I spit on them, the ones who educated them, on their mother and father, on the money wasted on their education. What shit that they don't care!'

Hurt as she was, she defended them. 'My children aren't good-for-nothings. The first is a doctor and the second is an engineer, they're not good-for-nothings.'

He bored into her, his eyes bulging. 'Wake up, you stupid bat, wake up. Your son Hussam isn't an engineer, your other one has left and isn't ever coming back. Your loser of a son Hussam takes after you: no brains whatsoever, no discernment, he's a good-for-nothing. He's penniless and all he can do is blabber. I don't know what he does when he goes upstairs. Tell him that he's banned from going up, coming down. Banned. Banned! You're also banned. Banned from going out: no more shopping, no more streets or walking around. And if it's necessary, I'll do your grocery shopping, I'll buy your socks, and I'll buy your clothes—you just have to tell me what you want.'

She spent her life shut up in her own house, knitting and watching television, rendezvousing with Vincent the heart-throb in her dreams. Like this, the years passed—or, rather, her whole life. A maid without a wage. And now, when she needed somewhere to run to, she couldn't even scrounge up half a dinar.

Crushed, she repeated, 'Hajja, I'll cook for you, clean your house, carry your bag when you do your rounds.'

'Shush, lower your voice, someone might hear you.' She remembered the lie about the woman in labour and tagged on, 'And there's the woman in labour.'

Um Azzam didn't seem to have heard this remark. Paralysed by her sorrow she said, 'When I think of how my life has been stolen from me, I wish God had taken me before I got to this point. Please, I'm begging you, Hajja, take me in.'

Sitt Zakia shook her head firmly. 'Your whole life you've been rational, clear-headed. What has happened to you now, my sister?'

Um Azzam felt her heart breaking. Her last hope of escape from her life had vanished into thin air. What awaited her now except a hard life, misery and worry? What about the kingdom and the crown? So what about loneliness when one wasn't married? Marriage itself was loneliness. Here was Sitt Zakia alone, living like a queen. She murmured, '*Mabrouk, mabrouk*, Hajja.'

Sitt Zakia placed her hand on her chest, letting her prayer beads hang. 'Congratulations for what? Why?' She looked at Um Azzam's polished pumps and remembered her own distress when her husband had left her and how she had then ran to her brother for help. 'What about your girls, Zakia?' Wajih had asked her. 'My girls are a heavy burden,' she had whispered, humiliated.

He had taken the keys to the old house, hanging on a yellow ribbon above the sideboard, and said as he gazed at the key swinging like a pendulum, 'It's true that the house is old and deserted, and no one wants to rent it, but if we fix it up, it'll be lovely. Take this key. Tomorrow, I'll send you the mason, plumber and tiler.'

Faintly, his wife then chimed in, 'Tomorrow I'll send you Azzam and Hussam, they'll help you move your things.' She had been standing by the sideboard, carrying the glass of milk that her husband usually drank before breakfast. Clad in a nightgown with lace, feet in shiny slippers. In that moment Um Azzam had seemed like a crowned queen up on her throne while Sitt Zakia was down below, much further below. But now the tables were turned and Um Azzam was telling *her* 'Congratulations! Congratulations, Hajja!' Oh God, what a traitor time is.

Weary, Um Azzam announced, 'If you force me to go back to him, I'll kill myself.'

'Keep it down, someone might hear you!' Sitt Zakia hissed.

The woman started to weep in utter agony. 'He beat me, he beat me, I'm telling you, he beat me. He didn't just beat me; he opened the door and threw me out in the freezing cold. He said to go back to my family.'

Trying to soothe her, Sitt Zakia inquired, 'Is it normal for someone like Wajih, so reasonable usually, to do something like this without good reason? Is it normal, Um Azzam? What did you say? Something about the children?'

'I said, "My children aren't hoodlums. You're the hoodlum and if they ran away, they ran away from you and I'm going to run away too." He started yelling like a madman and then threw the kettle at my face, and when I screamed, he started beating me, on my face, my head, my back and my stomach. Wherever I ran, he followed me.'

Samar sat with her head bent by the hearth, with Nuzha next to her, both eavesdropping. 'Not the first woman who's been hit and sure as hell won't be the last,' she whispered bitterly.

Um Azzam shrieked for the first time, 'Argh! Zakia! You haven't been in my shoes. If your heart was as broken as mine, you would yell at the top of your lungs and you wouldn't care who heard you.'

Pained, Samar shook her head and whispered, 'What good will it do if they do hear you?'

Nuzha turned to her and let it all pour out, 'I swear, if that was my husband, I would make sure that everyone knew.'

Samar thought about the situation. She asked desperately, 'But what can she do? Divorce her husband after all this time?'

Furious, Nuzha seethed, 'So should she go back to him and be killed?'

Samar glared at her. 'Where do you want her to go, Nuzha? Sitt Zakia's not going to support her and neither will this young man here.'

Hussam opened his red eyes, alarmed. 'Is that my mother's voice or am I dreaming?'

Nuzha crawled over and knelt next to his bed. She whispered tenderly, 'God protect you, you're just dreaming.' She turned to Samar and placed her index finger on her lips, signalling for her to keep quiet.

Sitt Zakia started up again, 'You remember how much Wajih used to love you and show you off in front of everyone? He'd only call you Jallab's girl. Jallab's girl did this, she did that, Jallab's girl has come here and gone there.'

Um Azzam shooed away her words with a flick of her hand. 'What am I meant to do with such empty words? All my life I've heard the same story, Jallab's daughter, Jallab's daughter. Whenever I said something, it was "Come listen to what Jallab's girl is saying." Whenever I went somewhere, "Where's Jallab's girl going?" When I wore a dress, "Look at what Jallab's girl has got on." They even stuck their nose into what I should wear and how I got my clothes. Just like he did: "This jacket, these shoes, this shawl, is from stealing and denying my and your children what belongs to them." Every day I would steal a half-shekel from his pocket. And the next day another half-shekel. This jacket, these shoes, this shawl, all of it, everything is from the half-shekels. Oh Zakia, even the house help has a wage, but me, I'm living off half a shekel.'

'Oh, what a greedy pig!' Nuzha hissed. 'He bought me such an expensive bracelet, and also a one-of-a-kind crystal chandelier.'

'Tell me what I should do!' yelled Um Azzam.

The two girls heard Sitt Zakia's voice repeat calmly, 'You've only got your house, Um Azzam.'

'He threw the kettle at my face!'

'Let's say it was cold?'

Um Azzam held her head in her hands, yelling, 'My God, my head, my head will explode!'

Hussam called out in anguish, 'Mother! Mother! I hear her yelling.'

Nuzha went to him again. 'It's just a nightmare.'

Um Azzam looked around her, her ears pricking up. 'Who's inside? I hear a man's voice!'

Sitt Zakia shook her head slowly. 'Not at all! It's the woman giving birth.' She was then overcome by a strange feeling of pity and guilt. She clasped her prayer beads and went back to muttering, 'Allah, Mohammed, Essa, Musa. Allah, Mohammed, Allah, Mohammed.'

30

Hussam looked at Nuzha as she was embroidering, like she did every other night. Days passed, weeks—three, four, ten—then months; he no longer knew or remembered. But now, comparing the past with the present, today's Nuzha with yesterday's, he knew how far he had come. Despite sickness and injury, Nuzha had been able to mature. Or maybe Hussam was the one who had grown up. What did that mean for her and what did that mean for him? For Sakina, this dishonourable house, the undoing of women and the environment? Who was responsible for the environment? Who was responsible for the depravity? The blonde, defenceless Sakina or Haj Iskander? Or the Palestinian freedom fighter? Which one of them hadn't done their bit?

He heard rustling outside and saw Nuzha's eyes widen with fear. 'I'm worried about you, Nuzha,' he said warmly. She looked at him, puzzled. He went on, 'If they catch me here at your place, won't they take you, too?'

She looked at him intently, still uncomprehending and unbelieving. For the first time she felt someone taking an interest in her without some sort of agenda. The human Nuzha, not the whore, Nuzha sans family, cut off from the tree. She felt a lump choking her, out of sadness for him and pity for herself; sadness charged with the situation at hand. Why was Hussam so pitiful?

Wasn't it tragic and regrettable that he had to stay in here in her care in a house that everyone was ashamed of, even her own customers, those who visited her in broad daylight? And here he was, sleeping and waking up in pain, suffocating from loneliness and drawn-out imprisonment.

A strong gust of wind whistled through the window cracks and keyholes. The poppy leaves heaved and bent over, colliding with the fence. 'Don't you worry, the wind's strong tonight,' she said with childlike cheer.

He turned his face to the wall. 'It's just . . . I'm worried,' he repeated. 'I mean, I know what to do if they catch me, I can handle it, but it's not your burden, not your promise to keep.' She gazed at him in admiration and wonder. Here was a man who, despite his wound, his bouts of fever, was still more reasonable than Asim, actually truly better than Asim; Asim her love, Asim her heart, Asim the nationalist piece of crap who didn't care about anyone or have any sense of compassion. She gave him love, all her love, a heart on fire, and obediently carried out countless orders. But she was no more than a number at the top of a list filled with empty squares and symbols, or, to be more precise, she was at the bottom. Strange and remarkable was the heart of a political activist, unmoved by the touch of love! Even she, even the whore, was able to look past the wads of cash. But as for him, he collected, calculated, beat people, made promises, assessed the weight of each fly, forgot about the human dimension of it all and then calculated some more. People to him were nothing more than chess pieces. Strange and remarkable was a political activist's heart.

'My aunt hasn't come back since yesterday,' he commented offhandedly. She slowly tugged the thread, her head fixed on the canvas. 'She has a delivery that's bleeding a lot; it's really gushing blood,' she whispered.

'A bloody delivery?'

She nodded her head uneasily. 'Yes, a very bloody delivery.' Then she raised her head and looked out the window, remembering his mother's face. 'All females bleed, all of them, I swear—girls, women with husbands, those without, all of them, I swear.'

'And us?' he asked, offended and concerned all at once.

'You men?' She examined his pale face and repeated the question in a confused daze. 'You men . . . ? Yeah, who knows? It's just that you men bleed from the outside.'

He smiled wearily. 'How so, from the outside?'

She thought, remembered, compared the two and became even more confused. Then she erupted, 'Yes of course! From the outside, and that's all, because your hearts are stone and iron . . . and we, we women, even someone like me,' she pounded her knee with her fist tight around the needle, 'even someone like me, you see? Even Nuzha, when she loves, she loves a lot, when she's loyal, it's to the end, when she feels, she feels deeply, and when she's in pain, it's intense, but all you men . . . .'

His heart sank through his chest and he felt it reach the bottom of his back against the mattress as he remembered Sahab, and what she had said to him.

'Come on now, Ace, you're still too young to talk about love. You remind me of my senior commander, who was in Lebanon before the civil war. I loved him more than my own life, goodness gracious! A woman to him is a pair of socks. Every pair is a different colour, every colour in a drawer, every drawer has a number and the dresser is locked with a key. He stretches out his hand to turn the key, opens the dresser, opens the drawer and takes out a pair of socks, the colour matching his suit that day. Then he closes the drawer, shuts the dresser, turns the key and walks away as if he's not weighed down* *by at all by his clothes, least of all his socks. And you've come to talk to me about love?'*

'I'm a small fish, not a shark,' Hussam had interjected.

'Today you're a small fish, tomorrow you'll be bigger, higher up. You've got to grow up sometime,' Sahab had woefully replied.

Breaking Hussam's reverie, Nuzha went on, 'I told Asim, "You're not thinking; even me, even Nuzha, knows how to love. Don't talk to me about the nation or history. I mean who's the nation other than you and me? We're it!"'

A thunderstruck Hussam turned to face her, her words hovering, going round and round, and he whispered in astonishment, 'I mean who's the nation other than you and me, we're it.'

She turned towards him, 'What? What are you saying?'

He smiled weakly. 'You sure know how to talk, Nuzha!'

She glared at him. 'What are you talking about? Of course I know, do I look stupid? Is it because I'm blonde, fair-skinned, friendly and living in *this* house? And even in *this* house, I'm a human being, I have a heart and a soul, and I'm terribly loyal to those I love. I'm human, don't you get it?'

'I got it, I got it.'

'You understand?' she challenged him.

He lowered his eyes. 'I'm starting to get it.'

'Okay, good.' She went back to her needlework.

He looked at the wall and the dancing sunrays, remembering the days gone by. He had still been pursuing Sahab, sitting on the green bench under the trees, confiding in the daffodils and lilies, contemplating the rings of light swimming in the forgotten pond. He had handed her a second poem. Sahab opened it, read it and folded it, the corners of her mouth upturned.

'Didn't you like it?' he asked her anxiously.

'It was so-so, better than the first but ...'

'But ... what?'

'Still not fully developed.'

'Which one? The first or the second?'

She reproached him, 'The ideas. Oh Ace, in the beginning I was the mother, and now, I'm the land, and tomorrow of course, I'll be a symbol. Isn't it right, smarty-pants, that I'm not the mother, not the land, not a symbol, but a human being? I eat, drink, dream, make mistakes, I lose things, I get agitated, I am tormented, I confide in the wind. I'm not a symbol, I am a woman.'

'No, you're Sahab,' he said, visibly moved.

She grinned from ear to ear. 'And you're chasing the horizons,' she whispered proudly.

'And I'm chasing the horizons,' he mumbled, bewildered, the light surging on the wall.

Sahab's ears perked up. 'What are you saying? You don't believe it? Why do I believe that you love me? Listen to what

I'm telling you. You can think that you like, maybe love, maybe desire someone, maybe rest your head on her knee, maybe you need her affection, so what? That means you love?'

Hussam shook his head, perplexed, shivering as if a glass of cold water had doused him, and muttered, 'Maybe I need her affection? Maybe I rest my head on her knee, and the symbol's lost? The symbol's lost?' A light bulb went off in his head and he thought, And what if the symbol is lost? 'If the symbol is lost, I lose myself. What's left?' He shuddered violently.

The light quivered on the pond and Sahab began to read, smiling. 'Better than the first and second, I'm no longer the land, no longer the symbol, no longer the sun, but I'm the feeling.'

'So that's the secret. If the symbol dies, the feeling is what's left.'

'Now you've got it—if the symbol dies, the sentiment remains.' He put out his hand to say goodbye and tut-tutted, 'What a loss, too bad.'

'What a loss, too bad,' she mimicked. 'That's life, that's the leader and the artist that you are, in a distant deserted world, where the people are far away, where their leader's hand is on his heart, afraid of the candle of freedom being blown out by the cold gusts of wind. In wartime, death trumps feeling!'

31

The alley was dark, so she crashed into him. 'Who's that? Who are you?' she whispered, alarmed.

He pulled the keffiyeh from his head. 'Don't be scared, do you recognize me now?'

'Ahmed? Nuzha's brother?' she gasped. 'You've grown up!' He smiled feebly and his pupils quivered.

'Come this way, the checkpoint is close by and the army's there,' she said hastily. She pulled him into a passageway; an eroded stone archway was above them, as well as windows lined with flowerpots holding cloves and fragrant flowers.

He looked up and cried out, 'Cloves? Oh God, how the days fly by. Do I even know when I'll leave the struggle?'

'You're retiring?' She turned to him and smiled, 'You're still young.'

'Who's still young? Even children, are they still young?' he said, despondent.

'Shut it! The army's here.' She shoved him into a dark corner and stood in front of him.

A helmeted patrol of six passed in full combat gear. She trod stealthily and observed them as they edged away down the narrow cobbled street. From time to time one of them would spin around as if stung, jump up, then sit down suddenly like a dog, fumble with the bullet chamber, direct the barrel up above, searching for a head or an eye or a large slab of stone atop a house. She came back to him. 'Hungry? You must be hungry.'

He was bashful for a moment. 'And thirsty. I need a piss and I'm dying for a bath. Two years' worth of dirt on me and I haven't showered. What I wouldn't give for a sponge, some soap and a bath as hot as hell!'

She pulled him through the dark alleys under the archways, one stairway, then many, the Saha gate leading to the quarter, to Sitt Zakia. She knocked on the door, opened it and entered with the masked youth in tow. The old lady was performing her ablutions. 'Who's there?' she inquired, her eyebrows arched.

'Hajja, it's Ahmed, Nuzha's brother.' As quick as lightning everything she had heard about him came to mind. Ahmed the child with no friends, Ahmed crying, dreaming of escaping reality to America with its Madonna and its Dallas, then the tragedy of his mother slaughtered in the square, and Nuzha left without anyone, cut off from the family tree.

'Ahmed? Praise be to God, He has blessed you! You've been gone too long, my boy, and your sister's been worried sick about you. Come here honey, you'll eat? Drink? Use the bathroom? Should I put tea or coffee on for you? Fry an egg or scramble it? Or listen, I'll tell you what, I'll make you an omelette with some salad. Go on and shower, darling, and when you're done you'll find a spread waiting for you.' The young man made his way to the bathroom with a knife and axe in hand.

'Hajja, he has an axe, and I'm concerned about Nuzha,' Samar said.

Zakia wiped away her onion tears with her shawl. 'Don't be scared.' Then she remembered the rumours about his mother and turned her head far away, looked at the mounds of the *tabun* oven and then out at the mosque. 'I know, my dear, who knows!' she whispered worriedly.

'Okay, so what do we do?'

'What *can* we do?'

'He has to go.' Samar stared at her. Spontaneously, both of them remembered a similar conversation that had taken place between them a few weeks before, and both women smiled forlornly. Samar stood in front of the window and saw the mosque's minaret, a sheikh making his way to the top, above the rooftops, the wind teasing his prayer beads and going round the edges of his jibba. She remembered Sitt Zakia's prayer beads, her unrelenting praise of Allah and his prophets, 'Allah, Mohammed, Essa, Musa, Allah, Mohammed, Allah, Mohammed.'

At that time, Um Azzam had humbly begged, 'I'll cook your food, Hajja, I'll clean your house and I'll take your bag from door to door. Please just let me stay.'

'There's no better place for a woman than her own home,' Sitt Zakia kept on insisting.

Samar looked at Sitt Zakia out of the corner of her eye. 'Hajja, what happened to Um Azzam?'

The old lady cracked an egg. 'There's no better place for a woman than her own home,' she retorted confidently.

'But he hit her with a kettle!'

She beat the egg with a fork as she tugged on her lip with her dentures. 'It happens to women a lot and sometimes not so much, but she just has to be patient and bear it. The men of the house are her protection and crown on her head.'

'But Hajja, a kettle!'

'Enough, my girl, it's done. Thanks to God, she's gone to her house and is protected. Take a plate, fork, knife, a bottle of water and the basket over there with oranges in it.'

'He had an axe in his hand, Hajja.'

'God will protect her, my girl. Here, take the bread.'

'But Hajja, what about Nuzha, she might die.'

'Trust in God and don't be scared.'

'But I am scared.'

'Recite Surah Fatiha and Yaseen. If you prayed, you wouldn't be so scared. All you girls nowadays don't know what religion or peace of mind is. Listen to me. Start from today.'

Samar's eyes wandered and she whispered to herself, 'We've really gained a lot from this omelette, and saved Nuzha from the axe!'

32

Just as Samar started running home, she collided into her brother Sadiq. He stood still, facing her. 'Where were you? Where are you going?' he roared. She looked intently at his red, congested face, his agitated moustache—she was scared for a moment. Her eyes left his.

'Where are you going?'

She remembered Nuzha and Sitt Zakia, Um Azzam and the tea kettle, the survey and all the women, their hearts crushed, and their Women's Association. She remembered that night, the beatings and moments of humiliation, the gap between her and her family increasing. Then the axe, the barrier and the stone boulders. Israeli cement barriers, even if freshly made, wouldn't fall like wheat chaff if sprinkled with sweet water. Sometimes death itself is sprinkled with sugar.

'Go on home now, go on!' Sadiq snapped. She looked at him a second time. She didn't feel scared; instead she felt the blazing anger of a volcano. She looked inside herself, down into her depths. *Twenty-six, twenty-six, I'm now twenty-six, and in front of him I become a baby. Twenty-six, with a degree, a job, publications, yet in front of him I turn to putty. Twenty-six and this young nationalist rules over the beast like a ringmaster. I'm the beast and he's the ringmaster.*

Samar's brother beckoned with his hand, his sweat increasing with the hot air blowing out from the nearby oven, the stench of sweat rising from his armpits. She remembered his baking tools, the large flat wooden peel he used to shuttle loaves in and out of the oven. *This baker, this labourer, isn't he the liberator of the nation and the class system, as Marx said?*

'This is necessary,' had been Sahab's words in the association meeting, 'but as for civilization, awareness and logic, without awareness there's no civilization, and without civilization, freedom breaks down.'

'And the class system?'

'A stone to build our pyramid, just a stone.'

'And freedom? The call of the land?'

'A note in our symphony.'

'And the groaning of the spirit?'

'The groaning of the spirit remains hidden if it's not revealed. Love doesn't equate to class, ready-made moulds and stores. We're not goods!' Sahab had yelled this and sang that, and all the women of the association marched out shouting. The street had been filled with two lines, a line of men and a line of soldiers; the women were beaten from both sides.

A passing patrol snapped Samar out of reverie. It stopped to harass all those present. Sadiq turned, patting down his pockets. Where was his ID? In his top pocket? In the bottom one? In his trousers or in his jacket? Samar looked at him. Good God! His gaze was no longer aggressive, he was no longer bothered about catching her in the middle of the souk, he was no longer the strutting stallion. He only wanted peace and security. She looked at him again.

'Sis, have you seen my ID?' he asked apprehensively.

She smiled gloatingly at first, then sadly, then weakly and finally patiently asserted, 'Don't you worry, I'll stay with you, I'll stand in front of you and they won't see you.' Stand by him she did, and the soldiers passed without noticing him.

33

'Nuzha!' Samar yelled, pushing the door. 'Nuzha!' She kicked it with her feet. 'Open up, Nuzha, enough is enough.'

Nuzha came out and told her off, whispering, 'Why are you so worked up? This isn't like you at all. I've got to go get him his medicine, stay with him.'

'Nuzha, wait, we've got to talk.'

Within seconds she had taken off, flying at great speed past the bed of daffodils, the lawn, the lemon tree, the gate and then disappeared into the quarter.

Samar went in and found him alone in the dim room. Their eyes locked and Samar unexpectedly felt his gaze pierce her to her soul. Despite his fever and congested face, Hussam whispered, propelled with desire, 'Come here.'

She drew closer as if bewitched.

'Sit next to me. I'm lonely.'

She sat down and, captivated by his eyes, felt a tremor go through her body. He adjusted himself and bent over, trying to come across as collected, but his eyes clearly showed his loneliness and distress. He motioned to his chest, 'I have a hole in my heart, an emptiness. You must have the same.'

And like that she felt the emptiness growing. It had always been there but it had never bled or even had the appearance of a wound. She immediately felt a drill boring into her, a fire between her ribs.

'Take my hand and promise me something,' he said.

Panicked, she trembled and recoiled. 'And Sahab? What about her?'

He didn't hear what she said and began to groan, 'My heart is in pieces. All at once, I'm close to her but far away. I saw her sailing on the rivers, the roads and hills of the West. Thousands of faraway lights in the distance and me standing here, saying it's my country but it's really not. I say it's my land but it's not. I thought she was light but she's fire. I wander endlessly, calling out to the wind, but my lover's heart crushes me like a cresset aflame. I say she was, and now she's become. I tell myself, she was there and now she's here. Who is lost? Me or my path? My path is long and forgotten in the depths of the earth. I am the abandoned and the one who abandoned. I am the beloved and the lover. Sahab is a mirage leading me on a magic carpet. She is the revolution, windswept. The Intifada stretched out by fear. I'm scared of her being lost and me losing myself with her. I'm scared of staying, of escaping. I'm scared the night will take me and I'll forget my promises. But if you promise me something I won't forget it.'

'And Sahab?' she whispered painfully. 'What about her?'

Feverishly he blurted, 'With me, you are Sahab.'

'But you're so far away!'

'No, I'm not far away. I'm from your country, your land, from the square where we'd get together as children and play, distributing leaflets, writing our names on the walls, chanting, "Long live the revolution, oh Egypt!" You understand, you get what I'm trying to say?'

She nodded her head. 'I got it. I got it.'

'And do you feel my love?'

Her whole being quivered. Painfully she lamented, 'Shame on you, here you are wounding me a hundred times over. My heart was calm and carefree. How will it hold up after today? I came to defend Nuzha and protect her from Sakina's stigma. And now I find myself in such a bizarre situation that I couldn't have ever imagined. Now, I've become the fugitive, not Nuzha. You've hurt me, and yet my mind wanders and my heart beats wildly, as if my chest can't contain it. Enough!'

'And what about me?'

'Yes, you're injured, but I meant it's not good to hurt others.'

'Aren't I hurt?'

She looked at him and felt the enormity of his tragedy. She remained tied down by his wound.

'So then promise me something,' he said.

She stood up in the room, unsteady. She felt the darkness of the room carry her to the deserts of passion. She ejected a tortured whisper, 'What is this passion? This torment? This burning desire?' She looked at Hussam's feverish face. In that moment she hated him and worshipped him all at once. 'You're the reason for my pains, my tears.'

He raised his black eyes and whispered tenderly, 'And it's I who'll wipe them away.'

34

The matter was settled. She was in love with an unattainable man, someone who didn't belong to her. For a few moments she felt guilty, then torn apart and finally completely destroyed. For her, the whole world was Hussam's eyes. Even Nuzha, even the victim and the executioner, even Ahmed, her harsh surroundings, history, the origins of the earth, sunlight, waves at sea—nothing could satisfy her like Hussam's voice. He stretched out his hand and whispered, 'Come here.'

She got up from her chair and came closer. Without planning to do so, or even thinking about it, she fell to the ground by his bed and buried her head in the sheets. The world turned, then crashed down and she still found herself captive to a great love.

'Never in my life had I thought of taking you from her. I'd always see you in the quarter walking in front of me, but I didn't feel anything for you. Of course, you were nice to look at. Why deny it? But you were out of my reach and she was Sahab, and everyone knows your story with her.' In his eyes, she saw his world shift. 'Everyone knows.' he echoed.

Light reflected off the wall, illuminating things down to their tiniest details. Stunned, he thought, *Was our story really that common? Was it a story, or a dream? Or a nightmare? I had never touched her, she had never touched me. I'd never taken her in my arms to travel the world with her and challenge the peals of thunder. She was there, and I was here. Two separate parts of the same body: the head turned to one side and the torso to the other.*

Stricken by the idea of stabbing Sahab in the back, Samar added, 'Imagine, just try to imagine if Sahab knew that I've betrayed her! Sahab's my sister, just like Nuzha, and all other women. You, you're a male in a quarter that worships men. Sahab's my sister, I see her often at the association, hear her speak about our current reality and say "Ameen!" In the association, Sahab, a lot of other girls and I talk about history, the effects of education and deception. We say that oppression doesn't only come from men—there are also women who eat flesh and throw the bones to the stray dogs. We women, we don't learn from what has happened to other women. We're always battling one another, killing one another to see how far we can push the boundaries. If I knew where my own borders were, I wouldn't have trespassed on another's. You are in her territory, not mine.'

'Am I a piece of land to be divided? No, I won't be that,' he objected in frustration.

'That's not what I meant, but how can we share you? The world's like that—destiny and what is allotted.'

'And who decides how things get allotted? Who's the judge? You?'

'No, no. Of course not. Who said I was?'

'Then the sheikh, or the priest, or the church?'

'No, obviously not.'

'Then who?'

'I don't actually know,' she said, stumped. And then she descended into a kingdom of silence.

He looked at the wall, the rays of light, shadows of the leaves, the setting sun, and said tenderly, 'I did love her, but I was young. For year after year I swore by her. I wrote poetry, stories, I dreamt so much and wandered even more. I lost my days to wandering on roads, hoping for the sun to rise while it set. I've criss-crossed the country, traversed mountains, and she, like the Pyramids, never left my thoughts. But I grew up—or, rather, my situation changed. Because of who?

Maybe Nuzha, or the events that pulled us into their slip-stream. Suddenly, we renege on a commitment we had made. What's more honest: that I retreat from a position that I no longer believe in because it has changed, or remain on a rope tied to an old building that sheltered me when I was younger? Even positions change, faces, history, feelings, commitments, everything. This is the world, it keeps turning—can we stop it? Can we challenge and deny the laws of change while we struggle and fight for the sake of change? Is this the oppression, the deception that you talk about in the association? Do you all want us to pause, stop the wheel of life from turning, go back and revive "fate" instead of "change"?'

She was completely silent but her mind was fizzing. Rattled, she looked at him. *What if he gives me a promise and breaks it in the name of change? What if he gives me love and it melts away in the name of change? What if I get caught up in the details of his life and forget my name for the sake of change? What if a storm blows and plucks his heart from mine? What will be left? Am I to wait for death, fear, or not exist at all? Fear is armour that doesn't even protect wise men. This is the solution, here's the armour: die alive, just stop living altogether, walk blindfolded, close your door, live your ruin and wrap yourself up in the blankets of death.*

35

Her passion for him flooded her, making her forget about Nuzha. She sat in humble contemplation, prayer-like, conversing with surges of feeling. Flashes of longing captivated her being. The future seemed full of different types of love. All her restraint exploded and destroyed her, only leaving desire and a raging fire. The world opened up to a soul mate, to meadows stretching to God with infinite colours, banners, shooting stars and volcanoes.

She didn't know how much time had passed. Hours. Maybe centuries. There she was by his bedside at his feet, sometimes playing the mother, at others the lover. Everything had a different meaning, with a different colour: the rustle of the lemon tree outside, the wind whistling, the birds twittering, the silence of the room, the light of the lamp. His breaths—rising and falling—made her fly about, madly, worried about him. She reached her hand out touch his face, his forehead, stroke his hair, pull the cover to his shoulders, call him the sweetest of names. Whenever he would mumble, she would imagine that he was dreaming, chatting to her. She'd respond, 'Yes, tell me what to do. Call me! Repeat it! Say something. I'd give my life for you, you're my love, my eyes, the thrill of my soul.'

Nuzha didn't come back. It was Ahmed who showed up instead and was exposed. He didn't come from the usual back door or gate, nor did he set foot in the hallway. He emerged suddenly, standing at the door to the bedroom, contemplating Samar sitting on the ground. 'Where did you come from?' she gasped.

'From the cellar, underground.'

'Why didn't I hear you?'

He didn't bother with her question. He drew close to the man asleep and stared at him, then tossed his axe on the sofa. Hussam slowly opened his eyes and asked timidly, 'Who is it? Who's there?'

Ahmed sat on the edge of the bed and hastily said, 'Listen. Listen to me and don't talk back. I've come to take you to the rest of the *shabaab*. Two of them are outside waiting for my signal when night falls. It's cold. Give him a sweater and some blankets. And a plank for him to lie on. It's a long way to the top of the mountain. There are soldiers scattered all along the way. But we know the ins and outs, the secret passageways. In half an hour or an hour tops we'll be in the quarries with the rest of them.'

She felt the world spinning. What? And lose her love? It was the first time she had ever touched a man, told him that 'You're my sweetheart,' sat on the ground by his bed, dozing without proper sleep, not fully cognizant, rocked by waves of feathers. 'I'm going with him wherever you take him,' she interjected in a determined voice.

Ahmed looked at her sharply. 'Girls are not allowed.'

'It's not at all like that. I'm going with him.'

'No, you're not.'

'Of course I am.'

'You want to be like Nuzha!' he exploded. Furious, he glared at both of them. The secret was out: Ahmed had been spying on Nuzha after all. The words echoed in her ears. 'You want to be like Nuzha. You want to be like Nuzha.'

Outside, the gate creaked, followed by the sound of a footfall in the hallway. 'Nuzha!' Samar called out. She made a move to stand up, but he pushed her back down and shook his finger at her. 'Shhh. Not a word.'

Charged minutes passed, until Sitt Zakia entered instead of Nuzha. Without wasting any time, she said at once, 'Nuzha's not coming. I've told her already. Now, everyone go on home.'

Samar left, and then Sitt Zakia. Ahmed and Hussam waited for the two young men from outside to come. It all happened very fast: the stretcher, the magical cellar stairs, the place for ablutions at the mosque, al-Qadi hammam, Al-Qammim, the Al-Addasi enclosure, the cemetery, between the graves, behind the rocks, prickly cacti, a cave, the meteorological observatory, Al-Titi bridge, Bleibus, low rugged rock fences, deserted houses, the hospital, a rugged path, then the quarries and the hooting of owls in the darkness.

36

Ahmed turned his face, confused. 'However you explain it, she blames me and you.'

'Who's responsible?' asked Hussam.

He didn't answer, turning his face to Mecca. He looked down at the city, unfurled beneath them like a carpet. The houses in the vast valley were small stones in the bed of a river. Facing them was the top of the mountain, where new houses had been blown to smithereens, seemingly reaching out to the lap of God. Despite the shelling and the fires, the trees were still verdant, the rocks still grey and the sky still blue.

The shadows of the two women drifted in Hussam's mind. Old love, new love, or maybe the same love: the land, nothing was higher than it. Sahab had laughed heartily, bursting at the seams. 'I'm not the land. I'm a woman: I eat, drink, dream, make mistakes, get lost, heave, suffer and speak to the wind. I'm not the land. When will you grow up?'

He smiled silently. 'Me, grow up? If the heart grows old, dreams do as well. If dreams grow old, they become rubble, no more than a marsh. I'm a lover of new horizons, while you'll always be a *sahab*, a cloud in my memory.'

Ahmed wailed, 'I searched for Nuzha but couldn't find her. I went from alley to alley. She's scared of me. It's possible that she's lost somewhere, dying of hunger.'

Hussam nodded his head confidently, 'Tomorrow she'll be back, tomorrow.'

Ahmed turned to him, beaming, 'And Samar loves you, you rascal! I swear she's crazy, why does she?'

'Because she's crazy.'

A mournful smile came to his lips. In times of war, death triumphs over feeling. In times of war, symbol triumphs over feeling. And he, Hussam was captive to this: because the bigger the symbol grew, the bigger the abyss became. As for solutions, or what is allowed, and the occupation, it would be apt to say that this was a time for crippling others; or, rather, of incapability; or better yet, of miracles.

Fondly, Ahmed told him, 'Nuzha used to take me by the hand, buy me sugar-coated almonds and chocolate. She'd say "Tomorrow we're going to America" and that there, there's no worry about being seen or known. I would say "*Love Boat*", she'd say "Madonna", I'd say "Michael Jackson", she'd say "Dallas". Dallas, my friend, in the flesh and on TV.'

Hussam nodded. 'Of course, Dallas.' *Dallas, yet another deception, and a young girl who grows old to be a spinster. In Washington there are senators, Congress and the navy while we're here, becoming old men, powerless fools. Show us the way, O Merciful One!*

He felt like taking off. He felt the world swaying back and forth. He was a boat rocking in the wind at sea. But his leg was injured, his heart broken. His outstretched hand to the horizon only grasped thin air. His life poured out on the roads, above the town squares, the caves, rock fences and the quarries. *Where is the barrier, O All-Merciful One? Where is the barrier, All-Powerful One? Every day a new injury, and the wheel turns, becoming more complicated. Where is the way out? Yesterday we were in Sakina's house, today we're begging Tunis, before that it was Beirut, and tomorrow your desert, O Mecca, and your streams of oil. All of you, get ready for the trip, prepare the Arab thoroughbreds. But I fear that our downfall will be worse than that of my nightmares.*

Ahmed roused him from his daydream. 'This barrier has got to go. Damn their parents, they've sucked us dry like a piece of gum. Enough! This barrier has got to go.'

Hussam turned to him and took in his face. He remembered Nuzha and Samar's chiselled profile. *Woe to you, today's generation! Don't lose heart, Ahmed. If only my leg weren't injured, if our arms were strong, if what we desired weren't out of reach. If only the revolution in El Salvador came to Syria, if only it reached Amman, if only Ibn Battuta never slept, if the leader wasn't ever satisfied, if the belly was tied to the vagaries of time, if there was a mobilization against the caravans of betrayal. If only, if only, one leg reached Morocco and the other invaded you, Iran!*

37

They searched for Nuzha everywhere. Samar went around asking after her, leaving no stone unturned. People's houses, between the quarters, in the alleyways, in the onion souk, in the Al-Yasmina and Al-Qaryon quarters, in the caves, the olive groves, the municipality park, in the valleys, the surrounding villages, even at her grandmother's in Seilat Al-Dhahr—her grandmother, who had been dead for a long time, so long in fact, Samar was told, 'Her bones have turned to dust.'

Someone said, 'I saw Nuzha working in the olive groves with the farm hands.' Another, 'She was looking for something to eat and a place to lay her head.' Someone else said, 'I saw her standing in the long queue out in front of the association, receiving charity: soap, and some flour.'

Some said this and others said that till Samar lost hope.

Ahmed once saw Nuzha loitering around in Khan Al-Tujjar while he was in a small posse of no more than twenty demonstrating youth in khaki uniforms, rubber boots and keffiyehs masking their faces. She had stopped, fascinated, standing behind the deep-fried zalabiya, squash jam and tahini-halva seller, who had yelled out, 'God give you strength and victory over your enemies! Protect them, O God! Protect them, O God!' People repeated just as loud, 'Protect them, O God! Protect them, O God!' He saw her eyes widen as their eyes locked, and she stammered, 'O God, O God.' He wanted to step out of line and say, 'Come on, Nuzha, forgive me. I've forgiven you.' But the army, the gas, the stones raining down from rooftops, and the children running wild like jinns stopped him from doing so. The deafening clatter of sellers scurrying to lower their shop shutters added to the din. One of the cassette sellers raised his player up high and the souk was filled with the resounding song, 'The young have grown up, oh mountain of fire, oh mountain of fire, oh mountain of fire.' Ahmed felt his blood ignite like a range of volcanoes. He forgot about Nuzha and focused on fighting.

Another time, when he had injured his shoulder, they took him to the hospital in secret. There, he had seen her in the hallway, with a bucket and kettle of water in hand. He called out to her, 'Nuzha! 'Nuzha! Come here.' When she saw him, she fled and disappeared among the visitors.

At last, Samar found her. It was said that Nuzha was in the olive groves of Achour, then Al-Makhfiya and finally Rafeediya. She went there and found her among the shepherds and the farmers, gathering olives and sorting them. The earth still carried traces of the harvest, with piles of straw and the yields packed into sacks. She quietly approached her and whispered, 'Nuzha, please don't hide away like this, let me see you, even if just for an hour. I'll explain to you, you'll explain to me, and we'll go back to the quarter, hand in hand.'

Nuzha's now-tanned face was the colour of the setting sun. She gathered the corners of her jute sack and said in a hoarse, broken voice, 'You forgot about me. You betrayed me. If it wasn't for Hajja, I'd be six feet under.'

Samar remembered what had happened and how she had flung herself at Hussam's feet, counting the breaths of his chest, and how his dreams had carried her on the paths of wandering. She responded, 'Yes, it's true, I forgot you. But just for a few hours, not for ever.'

Nuzha shook her fist in anger, 'Those hours, they were crucial for my life. They determined my fate. My life was in your hands and you betrayed me, you threw me away. For one look from his eyes you betrayed me, for a word, a whisper, a touch, a promise.'

Samar teared up, 'I'm human. Don't blame me like this. I'm not a liar. I'm not denying anything. Of course I loved him, adored him really but I didn't know where I was going. I mean, did he himself know where he was going? First he was tied to Sahab, and now he's suspended between two mountains, two fires, between a plane, its transistor and a broken wing. You think I don't know his deep, dark secret? His heart is soft and white like a cotton field but his tongue stings, worse than sulphur, and his head fizzes like a rocket. How can I forget him and his promises? How can I forget his dreams and the groans of his soul? He's tortured by a mind and soul tangled up in electric wires, lights and ships crisscrossing the western coasts. If he hadn't heard me, maybe then he would have grown accustomed to exile, fear, hassles, suffering. But he did hear me, and he knows me and reads me like an open book. He knows that Sahab and I are of the same fertile soil that gives crops, fruits and nourishes others. He knows and I know that the world doesn't turn like a wheel, and that time isn't a loyal friend that shares secrets of the unknown. He left, left me alone, hanging by a thread, my face flat on the ground, aching to hear his voice on the TV or the radio. I wish I'd never seen him or met him! If I could just remain a solitary tree, planted on a hill in the east that only knows its creator, if I could only believe that love didn't exist in the world and that I had never loved. You're the one who said, take him from Sahab, but here we are, I neither stole him nor left him. He's the one who took me and pulled me by the roots. And now I don't have the blackness of his eyes or my heart that is laid out on his walls. If only I knew where he went, here or there, into the sun, into the shadows, to the sky, on the earth, or to an airport, if only I knew. If only he knew. If only! If only!'

'That's enough, you mad woman, you fell for a man who was already tied up, like Marbout. Stupid woman, how did you ever believe him? Listen to me, the man who sold his mother, his father and finally the love of his life, tomorrow he'll sell you, too. Anything and everything for the cause.'

Samar crumbled to the ground, her head spinning and spinning.

'How did you believe him? Whether he's high up or at the bottom of the barrel, they're all the same, tied up. And you, you'll be attached to someone committed to the cause who'll sell you for a bullet or an article in a journal!'

Spinning. Spinning.

'Remember what Asim did to me, you fool? Never loved me for real, never married me, or protected me. I was passed on from one hand to the next. Look at where I am now, and where's he? I'm gathering olives while he plays king with his hook-nosed wife, and you've come to tell me to go *back* home, to the town square? What for? It's not a square, you fool, it's a grave, nothing more. And the barrier, dressed up like an ogre who devours everything that moves, suffocates people, deprives them of air and light. Or the checkpoint, with its flag sweeping the ground. People see it and stumble. They keep getting back up, saying, "Destroy them, O All-Powerful One, destroy them, O Guardian. Pull down their mountains, snuff out their light. By your generosity, O All-Powerful One, give us the patience to live through this inevitable fate." What fate? What light? What All-Powerful One, what Guardian? What rubbish! That isn't a square, it's a bunch of walls, domes, a place for ablution, hookahs and a chickpea seller. All of them, all of them are eyes. They all have black eyes, wide open, that only see my bad luck, my stupidity and people's gossip. Who comes out on top? Him or me? Who's the sell-out, me or him? Who'll be judged? Him or me? Okay, everyone must be judged, everything is taken into account, but why me in public and him behind closed doors? Tell me why. If Marbout wasn't judged, why should I be? And if he escaped judgement, Hussam sure as hell will, too. Everyone's gotten away scot-free, my sister, everyone. And you forgot about me, and betrayed me for a runaway.'

'That's not true!' Samar cried out, pained, her head buzzing, as if charged with electricity. 'He's a man, a man of the house. He's one of the masked men, injured, a fugitive, who sold his mother and his father, but only for the land and his love of olives. You see this land here? You see these olives? Who does this land belong to? Tell me.'

Nuzha squeezed the olives in her sack and shook it. 'The land? It belongs to whoever has control over it.'

'And the olives?'

'To the one who sells them.'

'And you, Nuzha?'

'I'm not Nuzha, I'm a journey of misfortune and shame. Don't call me Nuzha. I ask: Why did they name me that? For ten years running, you can say twenty, thirty, fifty, they haven't stopped talking about Nuzha: Nuzha's left, Nuzha's come back, Nuzha's gone up, Nuzha's come down. I'm not Nuzha. I'm a journey of misfortune, a wasted life. Now let's finish with you, what do you want from me? Tell me.'

Samar looked at her, dazed. 'What do I want from you? Sure, you're right, what *do* I want from you? If you don't understand why he sold his father, his mother, Sahab—the dream of his life ... it was to come back down to earth, to stop us both from dreaming. You don't understand that you're one of us and, no matter how far you go, that won't change. You don't understand that I was with him because he was with me, and we were with these people. You don't understand that the land belongs to the one who works it, harvests it and weeds it. You don't understand that the olives are food for the poor and oil for the lamps that light up the way to the mosque. That Marbout isn't Marbout, Nuzha isn't Nuzha, the quarter isn't the quarter, and that the checkpoint, the flag, the people and the barrier—we are all of that, that's how life is. That's history. Do you want us to be like the Messiah who never kissed or was kissed? What if he did kiss? Do you think there would be an apocalypse if he kissed? What would have happened?'

38

Shots rang out. A farm hand exclaimed, 'Disaster!' People scattered like birds. The army jeeps snaked round the hill and stopped. Soldiers in shining helmets made their way down. The sun reddened above the olive trees. The women farmers ran terrified to their sacks. Bodies doubled over under the weight of the sacks. These women made way for the gleaming helmets, the leaping young men and the flying bullets. One of them crouched down, another halted. A group warned them, 'There! Over there! Watch out for the soldiers!'

Stones zinged back and forth. The young women ran, zigzagging their way to safety. 'Come on now, ATTACK!' A tear-gas grenade exploded, then another, and another. Rubber bullets. Dum dums. Real bullets. More grenades.

A masked man bellowed, 'Move it girls! Move it, Nuzha, and you too!'

'Ahmed! Ahmed!' Samar called out.

Nuzha stood staring at the young men jumping all over the place, attacking from one side, defending from the other, leaping from one rock to another, farming beds, rock fences and ducking and rolling in the valley. In front of a cave hidden by an embankment, the army shouted into their megaphones, 'Stop! Stop!' Then more bullets, a chase in a jeep, and snipers.

Moments later the first young man stumbled. Injured in his neck, he rolled down the hill like a rock. A woman farmer yelled from atop a mound of soil, 'My God, my God, he's been martyred!' The screams of the other women farmers burst forth. Another young man turned to them and yelled, 'Lie down! You mad women, lie down!' A solider squatted on a rock and shot into the open crowd. 'Bombard him with rocks!' commanded Samar. A group of women close to him threw their cargo of stones at him. A group of soldiers surged forth. The women kicked them, beat them with their hands, planks of wood and olive branches. The soldiers split open their sacks, and scattered the olives on the ground. The women halted for a moment. Then they slapped the soldiers, scooped up the olives and threw them at their targets.

The sirens of the military vehicles down below in Touffah Valley howled. Toulkaram Street was brought to a standstill, blocked with a lattice of barbed wire and nails. Cars that were coming from or going to Jenin, Toulkaram, Anabta and Zouata were stopped immediately. Passengers remained strapped in their seats, watching the events as if at the cinema. A strange film unfolding on the hill, which was a natural backdrop for the events unfolding.

Ahmed, struck by a bullet, collapsed from a faraway mound, near the plot, under an olive tree, behind the houses and the oil mill.

'Nuzha! Your brother is down!' Samar yelled.

Samar ran as the women wailed, 'Oh God, oh God, they've killed another. Come on ladies, attack them!' The fracas resumed.

Nuzha made her way to her brother, as if sleepwalking. She found him laid out on the ground, his head in Samar's lap. On his cotton shirt was the picture of an olive tree and the outline of Palestine; the bullet was lodged in the heart of the country.

She knelt on the ground, looked at his face, his eyes. His keffiyeh had come loose. His lower jaw was slack and a red rivulet ran down his chin.

He raised his eyes to her and whispered ever so softly, slowly, 'Forgive me, Nuzha. I forgive you.'

She shielded her eyes behind her hand and raised the other one towards the sky. He murmured with difficulty, 'My precious blood for Palestine.' Then his jaw went completely slack.

A settler soldier with a grizzly beard and hanging curls as sideburns happened on them. He shoved Nuzha roughly and she fell to the ground. He slapped Samar and seized the corpse, removing the shirt with the map. He began to wave it up high, exclaiming like a lunatic, 'Look! Look! I killed him with my own hands. It's me who killed him.' He hopped from one rock to another, from mound to mound. He rounded back on Nuzha who was on the ground. He waved the shirt and pointed to the gaping hole like a crater with black dried blood on the image of Palestine. He stared at her with crazy eyes. 'Look, look here. This is Palestine.'

In a flash, Nuzha sat up, grabbed his leg and sunk her teeth in. The soldier threw himself on the ground, losing hold of the shirt. 'You bitch!' She kept clenching tighter and tighter while another soldier beat her and yet another pulled at her to let go. Tighter, tighter, tighter. She began to convulse. Her jaws fused to one another, tearing apart his flesh. The soldiers started to trample and stamp upon her, until she was nothing more than a pile of meat.

An ambulance siren sliced through the air. Army trucks rushed in and another jeep climbed the hills towards the olive trees. One unit searched the surroundings of the valley and the darkness of the caves. Soldiers collected their corpses and their injured, then got into the ambulance. The remaining groups withdrew, one after the other. Nuzha still lay on the ground. Samar approached, her face ashen, and took her into her arms without a word. The women farmers came closer as well and asked, 'The young man is with you?'

'Yes, he's one of ours.'

'Was he martyred?'

'Yes, he's dead.'

'Why are you so quiet then? Where are your celebration cries?'

A first trill went off, then another. Nuzha stared at the women. Dazed, she said, 'Get them away from me, away.'

One of the farm hands yelled, '*Mabrouk* Palestine, congratulations to you. You have a new groom!'

Practically seething, Nuzha whispered slowly, 'I said, get them away from me.'

Samar raised her hand and signalled to the women to quiet down. One of them yelled, 'Poor fellow. It's not right that a martyr is sent off without a celebration. Who are you? His mother? Sister? What? Curse the devil and call on God! Celebrate Palestine's new groom.'

Nuzha went wild. She spat out, 'Shit on Palestine! I want my brother, not Palestine.'

'Shame on you, woman, watch out for the devil!'

'Leave her alone, leave her alone!' Samar yelled.

'She must trill and damn the devil. How can she let go of such precious blood without a celebration?'

Nuzha leapt up from the ground as if possessed. 'I'm the one who's going to celebrate your blood, you bitches. I'm going to celebrate your blood, you old whores.'

They slapped their cheeks, flabbergasted. 'This one's off her rocker! God help you, Palestine!'

Nuzha stood in front of the sack of olives. She started to scoop them up and throw them at the women. She slapped her face, shaking with anger, unhinged, and yelled, 'Damn your, father Palestine. Damn the one who gave you life! Damn your dust, your land, your sky, damn whoever says, "I am Palestinian". You've taken my mother, my father, my brother, the land, the honour. You've left nothing for me, Palestine. What's left for me? No one alive, nothing in my pocket, no friend, no relative, they're all gone, all crushed, all cursed, all torn apart, hopeless. Go on now, go away!' And she went back to hysterically throwing olives at them.

The women retreated, aghast, slapping one hand against the other, aggrieved. 'Poor girl has lost her marbles. Only God can save her. There is no power but His.'

Samar burst into tears, stretching her hands out to Nuzha, begging, 'Calm down please, for God's sake.'

Nuzha waved her hands in the air. 'Enough of God, Mohammed, Essa, Musa, Red Cross and the UN. No one sees or hears. Since when has the world thought of us as humans? And he who's seated up there on the throne, can't you see Him? Why don't you call Him, tell Him, God, do you only keep an eye out for the bastards? What have we done? Why do you look at us differently? His eyes are looking out for the rifles but we are the poor ones without anyone in our corner.' Her eyes bore into Samar. She came closer and shook her violently. 'It's not just me; it's you, too. Watch out, you fool, don't tie yourself down to someone who isn't around. You think he'll come back? That he's well hidden and no one can reach him? That he's a sycamore tree planted in an orchard, there, up top? You think he'll come back in shape without crutches? Wake up, how can he walk if he's crippled? Tell me, how can he fly without wings or even walk? Tell me how! TELL ME!'

39

The alley was teeming with mourners and demonstrators until no corner was left unoccupied. The crowd made its way to the martyr's house. Sakina's house, a house that had been of ill repute but was now no longer ostracized by the quarter. Its doors and windows were flung wide open, the back garden full of girls. The young men and women stood at the edges of the fence surrounding the house. Flags fluttered; palm fronds waved back and forth; roses, lilies and wreaths of flowers encircled the photos of the martyr stuck to all the walls.

Songs and hymns saluted the perseverance and people of the nation. The applause rattled eardrums. Men who had finished with their prayers streamed out of the mosque to the house in mourning. Young men lined either side of the road clad in keffiyehs and military uniforms, leading everyone to the house with signals.

The square had sunk; it was completely bereft of people and jinns. The slightest breath of life couldn't be heard. Even the soldiers disappeared abruptly, no longer prowling the alleys in search of their next victim. They gathered on the roof of the checkpoint, above their flag, surveying the atmosphere with their binoculars.

Autumn breezes sailed through the alleyways, pregnant with the aroma of coffee and what was left of the other smells that had been accumulating till the midday closure of the market: falafel, *zalabiya*, fried sheep intestines, seasonal vegetables, spices, fennel, onion, fresh meat of slaughtered animals dangling over the heads of passers-by on the pavement. Carpets, cassettes, colourful clothes, handkerchiefs, the yells of hawkers, the voices of Raghib Alama and Um Al-Khal, revolution songs 'Fire Mountain' and 'Victory Generation': all fading away from Khan Al-Tujjar. All that was left in the square were worn, tatty sofas that even a thief would be embarrassed to steal. Left behind at the foot of the walls were piles of rubbish: cartons, rusty iron wires, trampled vegetables.

Sitt Zakia, with her bag in hand, tottered to the martyr's house, saying *bismillah*. She saw the deserted streets and imagined them full of jinns. The afternoon call to prayer rang out, resounding through the empty market. She raised her eyes to see a spiderweb undulating between the lamps and the ventilation shafts in the ceiling. The web was long, thick and old, seemingly there from time immemorial. The spider itself was the size of a frog and it swayed from hole to hole. Nablus was old, very old indeed, as old as time and history. She grew afraid and walked to the edge of the pavement far from the spider. When she climbed the steps to the square, she saw the soldiers, the checkpoint, their binoculars and their blue flag waving back and forth. She was the only one in the square, as well as the alleyways and the quarters. The mouth of the alley to the quarter was blocked by a ton of rocks that forced her to take a roundabout way to reach the house in mourning.

A young man called out, 'Mama, did you see soldiers?'

'I saw them, I saw them.'

'They've got binoculars?'

'Yes.'

'Are they armed?'

'Like always.'

'How many?'

'Only God knows, maybe twenty, maybe fifty, a hundred? I couldn't count.'

The young man turned round to his friends. She saw them climb over the fence.

She saw young men, women, flower wreaths, lilies, palm fronds, and Ahmed's photo in the middle of it all. She walked the back garden, the hallway, the steps and the entrance hall packed with people. She entered the sitting room but this time she didn't hear the chandelier baubles. She made her way to the centre of the room where the women surrounded Nuzha, who was cloaked in black from head to toe. Nuzha wasn't as she normally was, or that's how it seemed to Sitt Zakia. She didn't cry, didn't look at the women or any of the other people. Her eyes were fixed on a point high up on the wall.

Sitt Zakia sat down and sucked on some sugar-coated almonds, usually put out as a sign of blessing for a new groom, listening to the hymns of revolution and liberation. She recalled another funereal gathering, the day Hussam had come and told her off, the day she had worried for him, but he had brushed her off with, 'Is it me you're worried about or the house?' The day where the women in attendance had shared their stories and hookahs, remembering her stepmother, her history and her childhood. Praise be to God!

Even her, even Sitt Zakia, the old Hajja, mother of the youth, she had a childhood and a history! This thought came to mind when a new head popped out into the world that very morning, filling the room with his wide-mouthed cries. 'Shhh my boy, God protect you. Today I pulled you from your mother's womb, tomorrow the womb of the earth will swallow you up. Shhh my boy and don't tell. Or maybe, cry as much as you want, afraid of what tomorrow may bring. Is there anything worse than the unknown?'

She wiped her face with the edge of her yannis, turning to look off in the distance. If that new born knew what awaited him, he would have crawled back into his mother's womb! If he knew, if he knew . . . thankfully he doesn't!

Samar came and sat next to Sitt Zakia. She whispered, 'Where have you been, Hajja? We've been waiting for you!'

Sitt Zakia stared at her. Praise be to God, this is what she had been dreaming of—that Samar would be linked to Hussam and that she would stay in the quarter. Hussam had taken her; Sitt Zakia had made her stay here, as had her ties to the quarter—keeping her close. The other day she had told her, 'If you had married another man who isn't a fugitive, we would have lost you and you would have been lost: locked up at home, finished like other women.'

Samar's eyes glistened with tears as she smiled, 'Why not, Hajja? Aren't I also human, dreaming of a house of my own and a man to come home to me every evening?' Sitt Zakia had welled up as well but didn't smile. 'He still limps on crutches and his pains are only just letting up. He follows what is happening from a distance, without being able to come down here, or step to the border of the town to come see us. I wish I could give him a leg, how I wish I could give him a wing, I wish I could give him a pass.'

Sitt Zakia did smile then and shook her head, 'This, my girl, is your fate. Go on now, go see Nuzha.'

Samar drew close to Nuzha and kissed her. She pressed a small piece of paper into her palm. Nuzha unfolded it and read it without blinking.

'What did he write to you?' Samar asked.

'You didn't read it?'

'No, I didn't.'

Nuzha's forehead grew red. She stuttered, 'He s-says . . . he says . . . that Ahmed's precious blood was spilt for Palestine.'

Samar looked at her as if she was watching a volcano on the verge of erupting. She said tenderly, 'And what do you want me to tell him? To take back to him?'

Nuzha turned directly to Samar and looked at her through her swollen eyes. 'Tell him . . . tell him that your Palestine is an ogre that eats and swallows all in his path, never satisfied.'

Samar was startled. She didn't say a word. The racket and the revolution songs reached a fever pitch outside. Suddenly there was an explosion. The chandelier baubles knocked against one another. The yells outside were ear-splitting. The crowd swayed and heads popped out of windows to see what was happening. Gunshots. A yell rang out, 'A second martyr!' The women went running, the man reciting the Quran fell silent, the revolution songs petered out. A verse here, another line there, the band torn apart without any harmony.

Sitt Zakia stepped out with her bag in tow. She saw the martyr hanging on the barrier and masses of rocks. 'How can I reach him?' she stood asking herself.

'It's done, Hajja, he gave his life.'

A masked man, with a Molotov cocktail in hand, was giving orders, 'Bring the equipment and the saws, this wall has got to go.' The blacksmiths of the quarter, the road workers, masked young men and those without masks gathered amid the bedlam, yelling, 'Knock down the wall! Knock it down! Knock down the wall! Knock it down!' The drills, saws, hammers and pickaxes got to work.

'Come on, bring it down!' But the stone was as hard as the Lord's mountain, as Mount Thor and the Pyramids themselves. Bang, saw, drill, break. 'Damn this fucking rock!' 'What shit!' 'What a wreck!' 'What a trap!' 'What a prison!' 'One day strike, another day mourning, then days where the sellers lower their shutters because of the curfew.' 'Barbed wire blocking the street corners and the roads!' 'Strange flags fluttering over our heads!' 'And the blasted checkpoint like a knife at our throats!' 'We are the slaughtered sheep that ram, thrust at one another and spill blood.' Bang, saw, drill, break! 'What a prison, what a shame.'

Nuzha looked out from the window and asked, taken aback, 'What's all the racket for?' The yells of the young men and women answered her, 'Come on, come on, knock it down! Down!'

Tear gas erupted over the heads of the mourners and women. The saws raked back and forth, no rest. 'Come on, come on boys! Fucking rock! Hit it from this side.' Another shot, a new martyr fell from the top of the wall. Cries rang out, 'A new martyr, a new martyr. That makes three!'

'Climb up from here!' One masked man ordered another. 'Get on top, then run to the square and burn their flag.' They lifted him up, hoisting him up on their arms and then shoulders, in his hand a Molotov cocktail. He reached the top. A sniper's bullet pierced him and he fell on the rocks groaning.

'Next one, come on!' the leader bellowed. 'We'll keep trying to reach the top, God willing, even if every last one of us dies.' They hoisted a third, then a fourth, the tenth, the twenty-fifth. The wall grew even bigger than before: a mass of rocks and bodies.

The women applauded. Sitt Zakia yelled, 'There is no power except in . . . Let it go for today, children! Wait till tomorrow or at night when they're sleeping. No point challenging them in broad daylight!'

No one listened to her. They were overcome by insanity, the flag became their Mecca, there was no space to think of anything else, just to keep pushing ahead. 'It's now or never, either we end the wall or it will be the end of us.' From the top of the wall a young girl cried out, in her hand a large flag fluttering, 'Now's not the time to reflect or think. Get them! Get the blue and white flag! Get them, *shabaab!*' A coughing fit strangled her final words.

'Why all the commotion?' Nuzha asked.

Samar yelled back, 'They want the checkpoint and the flag, can't you see?'

'And so what? Why all the noise? It's got to be from here? Do they have to die like sheep? Come with me, I'll show you how to get there.' Nuzha took her by the hand, pushed another woman out of the way, then another, and another. 'You all, come follow me! I'll show you. You want the checkpoint? Come see. You want the flag? Come underground with me!'

She walked to the kitchen, then the storeroom, then the secret stairs in the cellar, the magic door to the square, and in minutes all the women bubbled forth from under the ground.

The girl with the flag fluttering back and forth made her way to the checkpoint with a Molotov cocktail in hand and matches. Sitt Zakia yelled, 'That nut has a death wish! Pull her back, hold her down. Ahh! She's dead.' She toppled next to the checkpoint, against the wall with the Israeli flag.

Nuzha paused in the middle of the square, following the scene, her features frozen. There were soldiers on top of the checkpoint, there were women in the square, and the young men were still carving away in what seemed like slow motion at the body of rock. Pickaxes, saws, drills. 'Why all the racket?' she whispered to herself. 'All this, all this for the ogre?'

She staggered towards the dead girl. The women were already around her and Sitt Zakia was at the ready with her bag. The glass bottle that had been dropped was next to the wall under the flag. She picked up what was left of the bottle, opened it ever so slowly and sprayed the liquid on both colours. She raised her hand up and stared at Samar, who whispered, 'Nuzha, you finally did it!' Nuzha nodded without the slightest emotion. She hissed back, 'Not for the ogre, but for Ahmed.'

Then she struck a match.